Déjà Vu x 2

Sandy Goldin

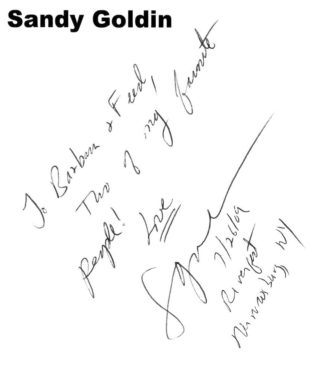

Copyright © 2008 by Sandy Goldin

All rights reserved. No part of this book shall be reproduced or transmitted in any form or by any means, electronic, mechanical, magnetic, photographic including photocopying, recording or by any information storage and retrieval system, without prior written permission of the publisher. No patent liability is assumed with respect to the use of the information contained herein. Although every precaution has been taken in the preparation of this book, the publisher and author assume no responsibility for errors or omissions. Neither is any liability assumed for damages resulting from the use of the information contained herein.

This is a work of fiction. Names, characters, places, and incidents either are the product of the author's imagination or are used fictitiously. Any resemblance to actual events or locales or persons, living or dead, is entirely coincidental.

ISBN 0-7414-5092-5

Published by:

INFI∞ITY
PUBLISHING.COM

1094 New DeHaven Street, Suite 100
West Conshohocken, PA 19428-2713
Info@buybooksontheweb.com
www.buybooksontheweb.com
Toll-free (877) BUY BOOK
Local Phone (610) 941-9999
Fax (610) 941-9959

Printed in the United States of America
Printed on Recycled Paper
Published November 2008

Acknowledgments

There are many people to thank for their help with this book. In my research, I was aided by retired New York State trooper Ben Johnson. Everything official that is accurate is due to his help. Everything that is inaccurate is mine. Call it literary license.

In the editing process, my colleague and friend Eileen Hennessey, an avid mystery lover, kindly offered her sage advice again, and I had two new helpers. My good friend Lynn Knight did an edit, and my good friend and neighbor Carolyn Steinberg did an edit this time also, as well as helping me computerize "Smith's" song again.

I would like to thank Karr, in California, for giving me my own two apricot miniature poodles, and for her friendship.

Finally, I want to thank my husband, Mike, who has given me new insights into love and relationships, as well as my father, Ned Goldin, for all his support generally; his lady, Vera Checcarelli, for her support of him and for her friendship; and my brother, Mark Goldin, for his continued interest in my work. And again, I dedicate this book to the memory of my mother, Eleanor Goldin, for the help and support she still gives me.

Prologue

I can't deal with this. It's too much—too much pain. I can't live this way. No one should have to live this way.

He looked out over the river that he had loved since he was a boy, but this time he felt no joy in it. All he could feel was his pain, like a knife in his side.

And the pain became so intense, so overwhelming, that it blocked out everything else but the thought of stopping it.

Chapter 1

"I can't believe it won't open." Marie sounded mystified. "I don't know whether to laugh or cry."

"Why won't it open?" asked Barbara.

"Because nothing's gone wrong yet today, and we're due!" said Marie.

"Maybe you blew a fuse or something?" said Allan.

"No," said Marie. "That was our second day out, in the morning, and it was the bedroom slide—it wouldn't close when we tried to leave. That was different. This time, it's making a noise at least."

"Slide?" asked Barbara.

"That's what you call the part of the room that slides out to make more space," said Marie. "It's the living room slide we're having trouble with this time."

Retired San Francisco homicide detective Jeremy Smith stood alone in the living room of his pre-owned, thirty-seven-foot Class A motorhome. He barely listened to the conversation going on between Marie and their friends Barbara and Allan Lynne as they watched him from the kitchen area. The Lynne's were good friends, but they weren't particularly mechanical, and he wasn't expecting much help there.

Actually, the primary reason he and Marie were here in upstate New York was for the wedding of the Lynne's daughter, Jenny. In two days, on Saturday, she was marrying David Mathews, her college boyfriend. Jenny and Smith were close—she even called him Uncle Jeremy—and so he and Marie had decided to combine their own honeymoon with the maiden voyage of their new RV on a cross-country trip. This was their final stop before heading back to Sonoma County, California to Smith's new teaching job in the criminal justice department of a local college.

Smith had resigned from the homicide detail of the San Francisco police department two months before he was due to start his new job. He and Marie had been traveling for four weeks, along with Smith's large black-and-white cat, Pickles, and two apricot miniature poodles, Chili Bean and Sparks, that they had inherited from a friend. Sadly, Marie's cat, Juniper, had passed away shortly before their trip. Fortunately, the remaining animals all traveled well and had not caused one problem. Unfortunately, the RV itself hadn't been as cooperative.

Well, he just had to approach this new problem logically. What was different about today than the previous four weeks, when the slide opened without a hitch? Oh, there was that case of wine under the dinette that was moved from under the bed this morning. Allan had made a special request for a Napa wine that was only available directly from the winery, and Smith and Marie had brought them a case.

Maybe there's too much weight on the slide.

"Allan," said Smith, "grab that box there under the table, would you. It's a gift for you anyway. I want to lighten the load on that side."

"Right," said Allan. He pulled out the box, "Oh, man, I can't believe you guys got me a case. Thanks!"

"No problem," said Smith. "Okay then, try it again, Marie, and keep the dogs off the moving part."

"Chili, Sparky, come!" said Marie, as she pressed the switch over the door.

"Oh, great," said Barbara, "it's moving—oh, no, it isn't!"

The slide had moved about two inches, with the motor making a sickly sort of sound, and then stopped.

Smith gave it some more thought. What else was different? He brushed his hand through his thick, black hair, with its slightly receding hairline, and sat back down in the driver's seat that had been swiveled inward to face the room. Even so, he had to weave his broad shoulders into the space. He wasn't very tall at five-foot-eight, but he was muscular and solidly built.

"Wait a minute," said Smith. "The last two nights, we dry camped."

"So?" asked Marie.

"So, we weren't at a campground, and we weren't hooked up to electric. We've never done that more than one night in a row before. And it's been raining, so the solar panel wouldn't help much. Maybe the house battery is weak."

"I thought it charges when we drive," said Marie.

"So did I. But let's hook it up and see what happens."

"No problem," said Allan. "The outlet's right here in the garage."

Allan was quite tall, and Smith noticed he had to duck his head under the doorway of the RV. He was what Smith's mother used to describe as "a fine figure of a man." Barbara was tall also, but her mother, Smith remembered, was short, and that probably explained Jenny's shorter height. Allan was back in a minute, signaling thumbs up.

Much to everyone's relief, it worked. The slide opened easily. Smith flashed one of his brilliant, full-voltage smiles that brightened up a room.

Barbara returned his smile, as most people were compelled to do. She was a strikingly beautiful woman, almost as tall as Allan, and her smile accentuated her beauty. Even so, she didn't wear much makeup and wore her hair simply, in a bun.

"Wow," she said, "there's lots of space in here now. It's like a real room."

Marie laughed. "Yes, it's comfortable."

"And I love the Southwestern décor," said Barbara, "and the solid countertops and nickel fixtures. And I can't believe the washer-dryer!"

"And *now* I can see how you manage with the dogs," said Allan, accepting a bottle of beer from Smith, who had moved to the refrigerator.

"Not for me, thanks," said Barbara.

"Me either," said Marie.

Accepting a glass from Marie, Allan opened his bottle, poured it out and took a sip, wiping the foam from his mustache. "Ah, nice and cold."

"Yeah," said Smith, smiling and wiping away some foam of his own. "The animals all love to travel, even Pickles. They don't get carsick. They don't chew things or scratch things. Poodles don't even shed."

"Miniature poodles bark a lot though, don't they?" asked Allan.

"At home, they do," said Marie, "but not in the RV. I was worried about that at RV parks, but it hasn't been a problem at all. And in the RV, they're with us most of the time, and they love that."

"So, Marie," said Barbara, "what did you mean when you said you were *due* for a problem?"

"I meant that, for the first two weeks of the trip, one thing went wrong every day!"

Smith laughed. "Yeah, the first day out, when we started to drive, the propane wouldn't kick in for the refrigerator. There was air in the line, and we had to pull over at a gas station so I could bleed it out. It's been fine since."

"The fridge runs on propane?" asked Barbara.

"Just when we're not plugged in," said Marie.

"Anyway," said Smith, "it was on the morning of the second day that the bedroom slide wouldn't close. That *was* a fuse, but we found a spare one in the glove compartment. Then, the third day, we were in Wyoming. It was May, but it was bitter cold there—below freezing at night. We turned off the water line to the RV, but the water hose still froze and burst. When things defrosted in the morning, we had a small lake going for a while until we turned the water back off, and we had to buy a new hose. The fourth day, the icemaker hose in the refrigerator burst, and we had a leak under the floor. Luckily, there was an RV supply store in the next city we went through that day, and I bought supplies to fix it. The fifth day … Hey, Marie, what happened the fifth day?"

"To be fair, nothing actually broke that day. That's the day you hit your head on an open luggage compartment door when you were unhooking us in the morning—"

"Oh, that's right. Good thing Marie used to be a nurse. It was a pretty big gash—lots of blood."

"Oh, my goodness!" said Barbara.

Marie rolled her eyes. "Do you happen to remember that I left nursing because I couldn't stand dealing with bodily fluids?"

"You did fine," said Smith, with a smile. "Anyway, what else happened on the trip? Oh, we almost ran out of gas once, looking for a gas station that could accommodate a thirty-seven-foot RV towing a car."

"That's before we found out about a gas station chain that has a special island for RVs," said Marie. "We look them up on the Internet now to find the ones along our path."

"And we got a roof leak during one heavy rain, while we were parked. I think that's it."

"Jeremy, you forgot the satellite dish! We were driving along a highway on a very windy day and heard a loud noise. Nothing looked wrong outside the windows or in the backup camera—no cars swerving or anything—but when we stopped at the next rest area, we discovered that the roof satellite dish had been ripped off. It was gone! It's a good thing no one was hurt. And it's a good thing we have a portable one also. Though we really reconsidered our plan to take our time on this trip—it was too much work for a vacation."

"But then, it all went fine after that," said Smith. "We've really enjoyed the last two weeks. Wherever you are, at the end of the day, when you set everything up, you're home. It's great to be able to leave the animals at an RV park and go be tourists. And the view through the huge front windows when you're driving—it's amazing. Oh, and Marie can get up whenever she wants to use the bathroom, or to bring me something to eat. It's great! The people you meet are great also. And I don't think there's much else that can go wrong."

"My goodness," said Barbara, "what do people do who can't fix things themselves?"

"They get professional help," said Marie. "And there's a club for road assistance."

"Enough of that," said Smith. "Thanks, guys, for letting us hook up at your house tonight. I feel bad that the park we're staying at won't have an opening until tomorrow, but it's the only one close enough to be practical."

"Don't worry about it," said Allan. "Thank *you* guys for coming all this way. Jenny's really glad you'll be at the wedding, Jeremy, and she's looking forward to meeting Marie. We already told her how great Marie is when we got back from my conference in San Francisco last winter."

"Thank you," said Marie, blushing. Her dark brown, curly hair was deceiving. She had her mother's fair, Irish skin—freckles and all—and blushed easily. "I feel the same way about you both."

"Allan, I can't wait to see her and meet David," said Smith. "I wish she were here now."

"She almost was going to stop by, but there's just too much to do. She'll be back here tomorrow afternoon. She wants to sleep here the night before the wedding instead of at her own apartment."

"She's going to be a beautiful bride. I hope David knows how lucky he is."

"It's the truth," said Allan. "But she's lucky too. He's a good guy. It's funny though—she's so short and petite and he's over six feet and gangly. And she's brunette and he's blonde. They should look funny together, but somehow they don't."

"And Allan and I are lucky also," said Barbara. "When David passed his CPA exam, they were talking about moving to the city. We were thrilled when they decided to open a tax office in town."

"Anyway," said Allan, "we'll be pretty busy until the wedding. Will you guys be okay tomorrow?"

"Definitely," said Smith. "Don't worry about us. We've already planned a canoe trip on the river."

"Oh, that'll be great," said Barbara. "Do you have a canoe?"

"No, we'll rent one."

"Why don't you just take one of ours? Allan, show Jeremy where they are. Pick one up here whenever you want. Or take it with you when you leave here tomorrow—make sure it's one of the two-man canoes! You must be exhausted though, with all your driving. I hope you have the stamina for it, even though it's a fairly tame river."

"Speaking of which," said Marie, "*I'm* really tired. I wouldn't mind taking a nap before dinner."

"I *should* be tired, I know," said Jeremy. "But I think I'd like to take a walk into town and look around. And I'm anxious to see the river. Do you mind, Marie?"

Marie walked over to Smith. She was just a little shorter than he was, but easily slid in under his shoulder. He put his arm around her. "No, you go," said Marie. "I'll make dinner when you get back. We can take the dogs for a little walk after dinner also. Barbara and Allan have such a huge property."

"How do I get there?" asked Smith, turning to Allan.

"Just make a left at the end of the driveway and walk back to the main road. Then, turn right. The town and the river will be about a mile and a half straight ahead."

"Sounds good. And don't you two worry about us at all. You've got enough to think about. We'll say goodbye tomorrow morning before we leave, and then we'll see you at Jenny's wedding."

Chapter 2

There had been just a few houses along the road until now, but coming into town, Smith passed a library, a town hall, an old-fashioned movie theater, and of all things, a pizza place. Now he knew he was in New York.

Smith rounded a curve in the road and stopped, mesmerized. About a hundred feet ahead of him, the road ended at an overlook filled with flowers, a bench, and a telescope, behind which opened up a huge expanse of blue water, rocks, trees, and blue sky. Continuing on, he realized that the water was a river, meandering off into the distance. It was the Delaware River, and it was as beautiful as he had been told.

At the overlook, Smith realized that the town continued to the left, following the path of the river. It seemed to extend about the length of two or three blocks—all two-story buildings with charming façades, decorated with flowers. He passed a post office, a coffee house, a boutique of some kind, and a supermarket called Walkers. When he came to a bookstore, he decided to go in.

"Hi," said the young man behind the counter. "Can I help you with anything?" Of average height and build, his medium-brown hair cut short, the man made a strong impression with the warmth and friendliness in his face. For once, it was someone else's smile that drew out Smith's. Usually, it was the other way around.

"No, thanks," said Smith. "I thought I'd just look around a little."

"Well, it's a pretty small space, as you can see, but there's a lot packed into it. Is this your first time here?"

"Yes, my wife and I are here for a friend's wedding."

"Oh, that must be Jenny's wedding. I'm Tony. I'll be seeing you there. And *you* must be the policeman from San Francisco?"

Smith smiled. "*Ex*-policeman. I *teach* policemen now. How did you know?"

"Well, I knew you were coming, and who else would be here two days before the wedding? You're in an RV, right?"

This time, Smith laughed out loud. "I guess this *is* a small town. Well, Tony, what can you suggest that will tell me something about the area?"

"Right over there, in the corner, is a section that covers everything local, even local authors. We have quite a few of those as well. And not that I'm trying to lose business, but if you're interested in the history of the area, there's a historical society inside the library that has a lot of old documents you might enjoy."

"I think I passed the library walking here—the green building?"

"That's it."

Smith walked over to the corner shelves and began to browse. He reached for a paperback. "Hey, Tony, what's this one—*A Death at Peterson Falls*? The falls near here are called Hunter Falls, aren't they?"

"That book's there because it's by a local author—at least he used to be local. But it's actually a fictionalized account of a local event. In the early 1900s, a man named Jack Hunter died when he accidentally went over the falls in his fishing boat. It was clearly an accident. He was fishing at dusk, looking for walleye. That's the best time for them, you know. Anyway, that's why they named the falls Hunter Falls in the first place."

"Oh. I guess I thought it was because of the hunting around here. I know Allan goes deer hunting."

"No, it's named for Jack. Anyway, that's when they closed the part of the river leading up to the falls, and they put up buoys and warning signs. So, Richard made up a story about a man who died falling over the falls, but he turned it into a murder mystery."

"I'm not much for fiction, and a murder mystery would definitely be a busman's holiday anyway, but my wife enjoys them. Is it any good?"

"I've read it. It's not badly written, but the locals don't care much for it. He writes it as a murder made to look like an accident, and it *is* pure fiction, but he even had the guy engaged to a local girl. Hunter was engaged. His fiancé at the time never married. They were a real love story—good people—and they still have relatives here who don't want people to think the story was based on fact. Actually, his fiancé was the one who started the library in town."

"Well, maybe I'll get it for Marie. And this one, too, for—"

A loud, piercing siren effectively cut off Smith's words.

"What's that," Smith asked, loudly.

"That's the siren that calls in the volunteer emergency teams—usually it's a fire or car accident, or an accident on the river."

"I hope no one's hurt too badly. I'll just get these two, then."

"Great."

Tony efficiently rang up the sale and bagged the books. "I'll see you at the wedding."

"Right," said Smith, with a smile. "I look forward to it."

Outside the store, Smith saw that a large crowd had gathered, and people were looking down the hill toward the riverbank. Smith joined them. He could see a collection of emergency vehicles and personnel, and for the first time, from this point along the river, Smith could see the waterfall upstream—Hunter Falls. It wasn't that tall, but he could see that you wouldn't want to go over it unexpectedly. Still, it could be survivable.

Smith turned to the young man standing next to him. "Do you know what happened?"

"It's Jason Berger. He went over the falls in his boat, I guess. Someone saw his boat going over, anyway, and then they looked and found him. I don't think he made it. It's a terrible shame."

"I'm sorry to hear it. Did you know him well?"

"Not well, no, but I do know he was pretty happy lately. He just started dating my sister-in-law's best friend's cousin. And I know he had a crush on her since high school. This was the first time since then that she wasn't spoken for—she broke up with her high school sweetheart. But, ya know, Jason fished this river since he was a boy—even at night, looking for walleye. And he was a cautious kind of a guy. He usually wore a lifejacket when he was fishing the river, I know that for sure. I guess this was one of the times he didn't. Still, I don't see how this could've happened. And he was so young. It's a shame."

Smith immediately thought of the book he just bought and of the history of the falls. This waterfall seemed to be the opposite of Niagara Falls—instead of celebrating young love, it was making a habit of breaking it up. "Yes, it's a shame."

Backing out of the crowd, Smith decided to head back to the Lynne's. As expected, the walk back seemed much shorter than the walk to town had been. Smith had this same feeling on any new walk—it seemed faster on the way home. Marie was sitting outside the RV with the dogs when he arrived. They barked like maniacs when they saw him, pulling at their leashes.

"Quiet!" said Marie, putting her finger up to her lips and speaking softly but firmly. "No barking! Jeremy, you were gone a while. I was starting to worry."

"There was an accident on the river. A young man died." He knelt down and gave both dogs a good petting.

"Oh, that's so sad."

"Yes, it is. Maybe I should tell Allan and Barbara."

"They're not home, and they won't be until late. We'll see them at breakfast. Dinner's ready, if you're hungry."

"I'm starved, actually. Why are the dogs on leashes? I thought Allan said we could let them run on his property."

"It's too close to the road here. After dinner, we can take them back into the trees and let them go."

"Good. And after we walk the dogs, I think I'll turn in early."

"And I'll join you!"

Chapter 3

Smith couldn't sleep. Something didn't feel right to him about that young man's death.

Maybe it was a coincidence—the similarities between the past and the present. Smith knew that people died on rivers. But these weren't tourists. They were local men who knew the river. And there was something else about it, something—

It's the new girlfriend, I think. If she was always 'spoken for' until now, what happened to the other guy?

And if there *was* a similarity between today's mishap and the events that occurred more than half a century ago, Smith suddenly wondered how similar today might be to the book he had bought for Marie.

Pushing himself up on his left elbow, Smith gazed intently down upon Marie's peaceful, sleeping face. Her eyes popped open.

"Oh," said Smith. "Are you awake too?"

"I guess I am now. What is it?"

"Sorry. I was wondering where you put that book I gave you. I can't sleep, and I thought I'd take a look at it."

"Do you mean *read* it? A *novel*? *Fiction*?"

"It *is* based on a historical event."

Marie laughed and pointed toward the hallway. "It's on the passenger seat, under my coat."

"Thanks. Go back to sleep."

"I'll try."

"Do you mind if I put this light on, or should I stay in the other room?"

"No, go ahead," mumbled Marie, already half asleep again.

Smith turned on the small reading light mounted on the wall on his side of the bed. He retrieved the book from the front of the RV and got back under the sheets.

The book was a five-by-eight-inch paperback entitled *A Death at Peterson Falls*. Flipping it over to look at the back cover, Smith read that the author, Richard Tomlinson, grew up in the next town over, but that now he lived in Boston. Opening the book to Chapter One, Smith began to read.

Carolyn Meyer was jarred out of a deep sleep by the loud knocking on the front door.

Oh, my goodness. What time is it?

She looked at the clock, and saw that it was 2:00 AM. She felt her chest tighten with fear. Her grandfather hadn't been feeling well lately, and he'd had a weak heart for years. But also, her father was a volunteer firefighter. Maybe it was a fire?

Carolyn heard her father cursing as he got up and went to answer the door. She jumped out of bed, cracked open her bedroom door, and listened. She recognized Jed's voice. He was a neighbor of theirs who was also the local peacekeeper.

Carolyn's mother walked by, heading toward the front room. She was fully dressed, her shawl drawn close around her shoulders. Carolyn quickly got herself dressed as well and went to join them. As she approached the group of three, the conversation stopped. Three heads turned to look at her. Three faces stared at her with concern.

"What is it?" she said, frightened again. "Is it Grandpa?"

"No, dear," said her father. "No, I'm afraid it's John. There's been an accident."

"No!" she cried out. "Tell me he's okay! Please tell me that!"

Carolyn's parents went to her, and both held her. "I'm so sorry, baby," said her father. "He's not okay. He's gone."

Carolyn couldn't breathe. The room went dark for a second, the pain shutting out all other senses. Then, she felt her heart close off from the world, like a door slamming, and the pain lessened.

She pulled away from her parents. "What happened?" she asked numbly, without emotion. "What ..." She winced as some of the pain pushed its way back into her consciousness. Taking a deep breath, she clamped down on it again.

"What happened?" she repeated, looking over at Jed.

"He went over the falls. You know how he liked to go fishing for walleye at dusk. We found his boat tipped over, at the top. We found him downriver a ways. He must have misjudged it. Things look different when the light changes. I'm sorry, Carolyn."

"I don't see how that could have happened," said Carolyn. "He never fished that area near dark. He told me how stupid he thought other people were who did—that the water was too rough there and you had to be able to see it clearly, no matter how well you knew the river. It doesn't make sense. He wouldn't have done that."

Jed sighed. "We fishermen can be pretty secretive about when and where we like to fish sometimes. Maybe—"

"No! Not with me. We were having a serious conversation. This wasn't a fishing story. Is that the only reason you think it happened that way? His boat was there?"

"Well—"

"Did you find any of his gear? He only used one rod for walleye. Did you find it?"

"Actually, we didn't find any fishing gear. We assumed it was in his hand when he fell in."

"Not even the bucket? Was the bucket in the boat? He always tied it."

Jed's eyes linked with Carolyn's. "Well, now that you mention it, the bucket wasn't there either. His jacket was in the boat, tied to the rail, but nothing to prove he was fishing." Jed paused. "Have you seen Walter lately?"

"No," said Carolyn. "Not since we broke up. He's supposed to be away on business for the store—his mother came into the library today and told me."

"Okay, then," said Jed. "I think I'll look into it a little more."

"One minute," said Mr. Meyer. "I just ..." He paused and pulled on his suspenders nervously. "If you're looking into things, Jed, I need to tell you something. John and I were having a beer after work last week. There was a little trouble in the bar with some boys from Pennsylvania. They were drunk and causing trouble, and John and I helped Marty get rid of them. They made some threats when they drove off."

"Okay then," said Jed. "I'll have a look into that also. Thank you, folks, and again, I'm sorry. John didn't have family of his own, and I know you were like family to him. Oh, and about his body ..."

"Yes," said Mr. Meyer. "When you're ready, we'll take him, and we'll bury him."

Carolyn started to shake in her mother's arms.

"Come on, then," said Mrs. Meyer. "I'm fixing you a cup of tea."

"Let us know, Jed," said Mr. Meyer.

"I will, sir. I will."

Smith's eyelids were drooping. He set the book down, turned out the light, and lay back on the pillow.

So, in the book, the boat is found at the top of the falls, not the bottom. But there's an old boyfriend in the picture here also.

It was odd to be reading this book on the same day as another boating accident at the falls. Just before dropping off to sleep, Smith made a mental note to ask Allan and Barbara what they knew about the original accident on which the book was based.

Chapter 4

"Regular or decaf?"

"Decaf for me, thanks, Barbara," said Marie, "if it's not too much trouble."

"No trouble at all. I made both. Jeremy?"

"Regular, please." Smith watched with a smile as Barbara filled two cups—his and Marie's— simultaneously from two different thermoses.

The four friends sat comfortably at the large, family-style, country-kitchen table. The kitchen itself was comfortable—bright and cheerful and apportioned with a variety of appliances that, though technically old, appeared to be in excellent condition. Smith suspected that antique lovers would drool at the large cast-iron sink. And the original hardwood floor was beautifully finished.

"You've outdone yourself, Barbara," said Marie. "To take the time to make crêpes when we know how busy you must be!"

"No trouble. I can make them in my sleep—they're Jenny's favorite. Besides, this is going to be it for the four of us until after the wedding. I wanted us all to enjoy the time together, however brief!"

"I like to cook," said Marie, "but crêpes are one thing I haven't tried." She looked down at the plate that had just been put in front of her, reached for a fork, and took a bite. "Oh, wow! They're great!"

Barbara smiled. "Thanks."

"Yeah, honey," said Allan, "good job, as usual. So, you guys heard about the accident on the river yesterday. What exactly did you want to know, Jeremy?"

"I'm not sure. Did either of you know the young man well?"

"Not him so much," said Allan, "but his family, of course. His mother's a widow. I went to school with her husband. It's a sad thing. I don't think she has any other family left in the world. Tom—that's her husband—passed years ago, and her parents are both gone. No sisters or brothers, I don't think. Barbara?"

"No, I don't think so."

"Anyway," said Smith, "have you heard any of the details?"

"Just that his boat was found at the bottom of the falls tipped over, and he was found at the bottom also."

"So the boat *was* at the bottom of the falls," said Smith, "near the young man, like what happened with Hunter—the man the falls is named after. But that's different than the book."

"The book?" said Allan. "Oh, you must mean Richard's book."

"How on earth do you know about that book?" asked Barbara. "It's not based on anything at all, you know. It's a complete figment of his imagination, but when someone bases a book on things that did happen, people are always thinking it must have some truth in it. This book has none."

"I have a friend who writes," said Marie. "She says the same thing—that people don't get it, how a writer incorporates known things into the background of completely fictional accounts. Like, when she includes characteristics of a few people she knows in creating a fictional person, the book character's actions don't have anything to do with what any of those friends of hers have done. But if someone thinks they recognize a few of the qualities as being like one specific person, they sometimes think it *is* that person in the book."

"Well, that's exactly the trouble here," said Barbara. "Jack Hunter was a well-respected—even loved—man, and Gwendolyn Gerber was the salt of the earth. I remember her best from when I was a small child going to the library. She was a good friend of my grandmother and like an aunt to my mother. According to my mother, she never dated anyone but Jack, and he never even looked at another girl. They were meant for each other."

"That's true," said Allan. "My grandfather said the same. You guys are from California, so you'd probably say they were soul mates, or destined for each other, or something like that. And that just might be true in their case."

"So," said Smith, "what exactly happened to Jack?"

"It was just a stupid accident," said Allan. "He went over the falls in his boat at dusk. Richard makes out in that book that a good fisherman would know better than to be up there near dark, but it wasn't until *after* Jack died that people started talking like that. It's a beautiful spot up there. There's a great view down the river and up the river. There's a calm spot right before the falls, before where they've set up the line of buoys, where you can anchor, or you can pull up onto the bank even, and just listen to the quiet. It's a place people like to go."

"What happened to Gwendolyn after he died?" asked Marie.

"She went on with her life," said Barbara, "but she never married—never even dated anyone else. My mother always said Gwennie had already had her love, and she'd wait until it was her time to catch up with him. But Gwen was never bitter or angry. She cared about people, especially children. She started the library in this town, the first in the entire area. People came from miles away to use it. She really was an angel. She never spoke a harsh word. She only ever saw the best in people. You know, it's funny, but

Beth—the girl that was dating Jason—she always kind of reminded me of Gwen, she's that good."

"I heard that Beth had been dating someone else from high school until just recently," said Smith.

"Well, yes," said Barbara, "Arthur Walker. His family owns the market in town."

Smith nodded. "I saw it."

"And you know, if I thought anyone would be her soul mate, it would have been him. But for whatever reason, it didn't work out. They broke up a couple of months ago, I think. I don't really know Jason well, but I've heard he was a nice boy too—sensitive—so perhaps *he* was her soul mate and this really *is* history repeating itself."

"Like déjà vu," said Allan.

"Well," said Smith, "there are some things that sound like the past and some that sound more like the book, so it's kind of like a double déjà vu."

"Déjà vu all over again!" said Marie.

"Déjà vu times two!" said Barbara.

They all laughed, and then stopped, looking guiltily around at each other.

"Why are you so curious about all of this, Jeremy?" asked Allan. "Are you bored on your vacation, or maybe missing your old job already?"

"No, it's just that … oh, I don't know. It seems like, if someone had read that book—and maybe they saw the same similarities between all these people that we're talking about—then maybe they would get the same idea as in the book, to make a murder look like an accident. Do either of you know who's in charge of the investigation, if there even is one?"

"I'm not sure I like that idea," said Barbara, "because the implication would be that it was Arthur, which is impossible. I'm telling you that right now, Jeremy. He doesn't have a mean bone in his body. He's smart and levelheaded and witty and kind, always with a twinkle in his eye. And *he* was the one who let Beth get away—he wasn't ready to settle down, or something foolish like that—though she technically broke up with him. But actually, I do know who's looking into it."

"Barbara knows everyone," said Allan.

"Well, I know *this* person. It's Bob Penny. Allan, y*ou* know—Maggie's husband. Bob's not a local boy, but Maggie is the daughter of one of my best friends. Did you want to talk to him, Jeremy? They'll be at the wedding, but why don't I give him a call? You could talk to him today, I bet. He already knows about you. He was looking forward to meeting you. He has a friend on the San Francisco police force who spoke highly of you to him."

"Oh, really. Who?"

"I don't know. You'll have to ask him."

"Well, Marie and I are moving the RV over to the park at eleven. Maybe he'd have time to have lunch with me, or else after lunch."

"He's a state trooper—or actually an investigator is his title," said Barbara. "I'll give him a call to see if he's at the barracks in town today and we'll find out."

Chapter 5

Outside the door of the River Café, Smith hesitated.

What am I doing here, exactly? he thought. *This has nothing to do with me. I don't even live here. Maybe Allan is right. Maybe I'm nervous about my career change, and this is a way to hold on to the past. Well, I never could resist a good puzzle, and I'm here now, anyway. I might as well go on in.*

As soon as he opened the door, the waitress grabbed a menu and walked up to him. She was a very short, middle-aged woman, slim and energetic, and seemingly very down-to-earth.

"One?" she asked, with a smile.

"No," said Smith, smiling back. "I'm meeting Bob Penny. Is he here yet?"

"Oh, you must be Mr. Smith. Bob's outside. Follow me."

The waitress led Smith out onto a patio overlooking the river. It was a beautiful spot. He just had time to notice that all the tables were taken when he heard his name.

"Jeremy!"

Smith turned toward the voice on his left. The man facing him, his hand outstretched, was quite tall—as tall as

Smith's good friend and ex-colleague in San Francisco, Lt. Kelly, but not as gangly, and he had very short, dark-blonde hair. He was also a lot younger, of course, being the same generation as Allan and Barbara's daughter. Smith noticed that he was in plain clothes—no uniform. Smith shook his hand.

"Hello, Bob. It's nice of you to give me some of your time on such short notice."

"No problem," said Penny, with a smile. "I was looking forward to talking with you at the wedding anyway. And given your reputation, if you have something to say about this situation, I certainly at least want to hear it. Let's get our order in, and you can tell me about it." He had to raise his hand a few times before the waitress came over. "Laverne, you busy thing, I'm ready for my burger and fries, and Jeremy ...?"

Smith had looked over the menu quickly and was ready also. "I'll have the salmon patty, thanks."

Laverne took the menus and left.

"About that reputation business," said Smith, "who is it that you know in the San Francisco PD?"

"No, not me. My supervisor. I don't know exactly. I'll ask him and tell you Saturday. So, just what are you thinking?"

"Well, I'm not sure why I have to stick my two cents in, but it was the timing I think. I had just been told the story of how Hunter Falls got its name, and about the book Richard Tomlinson wrote, and then I was standing next to someone who told me a little about the young man—about Jason Berger. It all just came together."

"Well, all I know about the name Hunter Falls is that someone named Hunter died there, but there've been many other accidents since then, over the years. And I'm not sure which book you mean."

"Oh," said Smith. "I forgot that Allan told me you didn't grow up here. And you were never a tourist here, either, I don't suppose, so it must never have come up. Jack Hunter went over the falls in his boat. He was engaged to someone named Gwen, who ended up starting the library in town."

"Oh, that's right. Gwendolyn Gerber. I know about *her*. I never met her, though. Before my time."

"Anyway, Tomlinson wrote a fictional story about someone who died going over the falls. In the book, the boat was found still at the top, which is different than with Jack Hunter, and I guess different than what happened yesterday. But also, the victim in the book had just started dating someone who was his soul mate and who had just broken up with someone else, which doesn't match the Hunter situation, but it *does* match with yesterday's young man—Jason Berger. And Tomlinson made it a murder disguised as an accident."

"I see the similarity, but still—"

"Yes, I know. But also, the man I was standing with on the bank—he was surprised. He said that Jason was someone who had fished this river since he was a child, and that he usually wore a life jacket. He also said that, nowadays, it was usually tourists who got hurt at the falls. I just thought there was enough to …"

Smith hesitated, noticing that Penny had started to fidget a little, and that he was looking down at the table. Smith sighed. "I guess I just thought someone besides me needed to hear all of this put together, and maybe needed to look into it, just to be sure. And I guess there's nothing unusual you've found or anything, so I'm probably just blowing smoke. Sorry."

"No, don't be sorry." Penny paused. "Look, I maybe shouldn't be telling you this, but something *doesn't* seem quite right. First off, someone saw the boat go over the falls—it was empty. So we assumed Jason must have fallen out of the boat, hit his head, and gone over the falls separately, maybe unconscious. But his injuries don't quite add up. It's hard to tell of course—there'd be lots of bruising from the rocks. But there seems to be one head injury that's different. And that's interesting, what you told me, that he usually wore a life jacket. Also …" Penny hesitated.

"Look, Bob, I understand if you can't give me details of the case."

"No, I think it's okay. I wouldn't mind your input. Also, we found one item of his clothing on the bank above the falls. Some of his things were found loose in the water— his jacket, his baseball cap, his fishing rod. But we found his shoes on the bank. That was odd."

"I see," said Smith. "That *is* odd, that he would be in his boat without his shoes. So, maybe he wasn't in his boat."

"Or maybe he liked to fish barefoot! Anyway, I want to thank you for getting in touch with me."

"It sounds like you didn't need me to. You were already looking into things."

"No, it was helpful to hear what you had to say. It puts things in a context, if you get my meaning. It tells me something about the situation that might help to explain it. And who was this guy you talked to on the bank? *I'd* like to talk to him!"

Smith laughed. "I don't know. He was average height and build, brown eyes, late-twenties. His sister-in-law's friend was someone's cousin, I think, or something."

"That covers about everyone in this town. Anyway, maybe I'll find him."

Laverne walked up to the table with two plates in her hand.

"I forgot to ask if you wanted anything to drink," she said to Smith as she set the plates down.

"This water's fine for me, thanks."

"Enjoy your meal." Laverne smiled and left.

"Well," said Penny, "the food's good here, so I hope you like it."

"It looks great."

"And to change the subject, my wife's anxious to meet you also. We hear that you write songs, and one is going to be in a movie."

"I guess Allan and Barbara have been acting as my publicity agent in town!"

Penny laughed. "Well, my wife, Maggie, believe it or not, teaches an acting class. She's a local girl, but she went away to college and was a drama major. She even worked in some summer stock productions. Anyway, I'm warning you, she's hoping to talk to you about "the business.""

"I'll be happy to talk to her, but I don't know much about it. All I did was write a song that one of Marie's clients liked—a lawyer whose finances Marie manages—and the client knew this director. Anyway, Marie and I are going on the river this afternoon, but the wedding's tomorrow. Is that soon enough?"

"That's plenty soon enough. But don't let her chew your ear off about it." Penny looked at his watch. "Although, I look forward to talking to you some more at the wedding myself. I'd like to hear about police work in San Francisco. But unfortunately, I've got to get back to work now." He slid his chair back and stood up.

"We've got a date," said Smith, wiping the last crumbs from his mouth. "And Bob, this lunch is on me."

"No," said Penny, "it's already taken care of. Don't rush off. Get some coffee or something and look at the view. I'll see you tomorrow."

"Thanks." Smith's goodbye smile was matched by one of Penny's, and he left.

Smith decided he *would* order a cup of coffee. The table he was at overlooked the river, but the conversation had taken all of his attention and he hadn't had a chance to enjoy the view.

It would be hard to decide what one thing made this area beautiful—there were so many things. He had been told that the Catskill Mountains weren't that high—and maybe they weren't the Rockies—but they were still majestic, and a lot greener and wetter than Colorado in the summer. And this river was special. It had width—Smith estimated that it was at least eighty to a hundred feet wide at this point—yet it curved in and out as if it were a sprightly stream, meandering into the distance, bordered on both sides by hills that were cloaked with trees.

Smith also had been told that bald eagles congregated here, and he took a moment to search the skies. Some larger birds flew by, but he recognized them as turkey vultures by the "v" in their wing pattern.

After a few moments, he gave up, deciding he couldn't wait another minute to get out on the river. He threw down a couple of dollars toward the tip and left for the RV park to pick up Marie and the two-man canoe they had borrowed from Allan and Barbara.

Chapter 6

"This is amazing!" There had been a smile plastered on Smith's face for the past half hour.

Marie laughed. It must have been about the fourth time he had expressed himself in this way. "Yes, it's very beautiful."

Smith and Marie had taken the canoe to an access point on the river about five miles above the falls. They currently were paddling their way down toward another access point just before the falls. When they got there, they would call the park on their cell phone, and someone would come and take them back to their car. It was just about a seven-minute drive, but they were told to allow two hours for the canoe trip downriver.

"I know I keep saying that," said Smith, "But I didn't realize how beautiful this area and this river were—I wasn't expecting this much, I think. When that eagle flew overhead—man, I could see his eyes! That was so cool!"

"It was one of my life highlights too, I think. What is it about eagles? It feels like we've been granted an audience with a king. They're so beautiful also, with the white head against the dark body. And when he turned around and flew back over us a second time…"

"Yeah! It was great. But I was worried this river would seem tame to you, after all the white water rafting you've done."

"It *is* tame, but it's beautiful …" Marie paused and looked around. "It's just a different type of experience, and we still have to keep our eyes open, like right here!"

They navigated around a bubbling area of protruding rocks in the center of the current, having to head over toward the right bank and back again. Smith sat in the back of the canoe and Marie sat up front. It had taken about fifteen minutes for them to work out a good communication between them—they hadn't been in a canoe together before—but they found that they were as much in sync with this activity as they were in the rest of their lives.

They continued along peacefully for another half hour or so on this wide and winding river that was bordered on both sides by woods and meadows. The temperature was perfect. There were no bugs. It wasn't the weekend, so they only rarely passed another person on the river or on the bank.

"What's that up ahead?" said Marie.

Smith looked past her about 100 yards downstream. "It looks like something floating—maybe a log?"

"No, it's moving from one side to the other. I think it's a small animal swimming."

Smith got an uneasy feeling. The object didn't look right. Every now and then, more of it bobbed out of the water and he got a sense of the length of it. It wasn't a small animal. It was disturbingly close to the size of a human body. He suddenly wondered if Jason had been alone in that boat yesterday.

"Marie, hold up a minute—Oh!"

"Oh my God," said Marie, "it's a deer! That was its head above the water. It's swimming across the river! I didn't know they did that. Look, it's getting out."

Smith laughed to himself at how jumpy he had been and at how he seemed to be seeing dead bodies everywhere now.

The deer made its way up onto the bank just as they came abreast of it. It shook itself off, gave them one glance, and seemed to levitate straight up into the air before leaping off into the trees.

"Well, life memory number two on this river trip," said Marie. She looked back at Smith with the same smile now plastered on her face. They took a moment to look deeply into each other's eyes, to fully share the experience, before Marie turned back and they continued on their way, paddling and resting and breathing in the day.

"Oh," said Smith, "there's the log cabin with the white barn. We must be almost there."

Marie looked at her watch. "But it's only been an hour and a half. I don't want to stop. This is great."

"I don't think we want to go over the falls, so I guess we'll have to pull over. Look, there's the warning sign. And there's the meadow on the left with the red pole."

Smith and Marie maneuvered the canoe over toward the bank. As they approached it, Smith jumped out and pulled the canoe partway onto the land. Marie jumped out and helped him carry it in toward the parking area. There weren't any cars parked there.

"Well," said Smith, "I guess we were lucky. Even though it's not the weekend, I still expected more people. Can I have that bottle of water when you're done?"

Marie finished her gulp and handed the bottle to Smith. "Shall I call the RV park now?"

"Hold off a minute. I think it was somewhere around here that they found Jason Berger's shoes. I thought I'd look around a little."

"Jeremy—"

"I know. We're on vacation. I'd kind of like to see the falls from this side anyway, though, wouldn't you?"

Marie scrunched up her face. "Actually, yes I would."

"Let's just walk along the bank a short ways. It gets higher up ahead and the view must be good."

Turning downstream again, they made their way along the bank. The parking lot was all blacktop and mown grass, but now they entered a wooded area and walked along a dirt path. Smith kept his eyes mostly down, scanning the ground and the underbrush along the sides. In a minute, they were out in the open again. Ahead was a chain link fence, with a sign warning people not to walk any further along the bank. But the fence and the sign didn't block the view of the river, which moved off to the right at this point.

"Oh, man!" said Smith.

"Life memory number three," said Marie. "What a view. That's what I call meandering! This river is an expert at it. And look how cute the town looks. I didn't realize how close we were."

"And the sound of the falls is so close too, with the spray coming up. It's not very high, I know, but it sounds … I don't know what."

"Exciting. Strong. Clean."

"Yes, all of that."

The two stood there for a few moments, arm in arm.

"Well," said Smith, with a sigh. "I haven't seen anything unusual around here—no sign of a struggle or anything. I guess it's time to make that call and head back."

Marie took out her cell phone. "Hey, there's no service."

"Maybe it's the trees. It works at the RV. Let's go back to the parking area."

They turned and walked back into the trees. By force of habit, Smith's eyes continued to scan the ground. The path was rocky, and on either side there were fallen branches and lots of underbrush. Suddenly, in an area of tall ferns on his right, Smith saw a glint of metal and stopped, placing his hand on Marie's shoulder.

"Hold on a minute. Do you have a pen?" Smith reached for the pen Marie held out to him, and kneeling down, he carefully pushed aside some of the ferns.

"What is it?" asked Marie.

"It's a hammer. Hold on. There's something on the head, something dried on it. And something else—it looks like … like hair, I think, stuck on it." Smith took a deep breath and let it out. "It's probably nothing, but I think we should get Bob Penny up here to look at it. I hate to leave this spot. Can you walk ahead and try the phone? Here's his number." Smith retrieved a small piece of paper from his wallet.

Marie walked ahead about one hundred feet, into the open, and tried the phone. "Still no service," she called back to Smith.

"Well, I don't want to leave this spot, and I certainly don't want to leave you here alone." Smith got very quiet.

"What are you thinking?" asked Marie.

"I hate to ask you, but how would you feel about walking the two or three blocks into town? I know we're on vacation—"

"On our *honeymoon*!"

"Yes, I know. That's why I hate—"

"No," Marie said, with a sigh. "I understand. Really, I can do it. Is there a pay phone there if the cell still doesn't work?"

"Go to the bookstore. Tell the owner who you are. His name is Tony. He's a friend of Jenny's, and he knows all about us. He'll let you use the phone."

"Okay. Off I go."

Chapter 7

Smith watched Marie walk off through the trees and down the driveway, toward the road. He took a deep breath and looked around.

There didn't seem to be any sign of a struggle here either. If the hammer had anything to do with Jason Berger's death, Smith didn't think it was used here. Why would the killer, if there was one, leave it in the same general area as the murder?

Marie's backpack caught Smith's eye. She didn't take it with her. He remembered her saying that she was bringing that book along, in case she had time to start reading it.

Well, I've got nothing better to do, he thought, reaching into the backpack. He found the place where he had left off, but decided to flip to the back of the book instead, looking for more information about the fictional murder. He found a promising phrase and began to read.

... didn't make sense to her. She turned away from the river and walked back to the road.

How could John die this way? It wasn't possible, but no one would believe her. And they didn't even listen to her. They talked about those kids at the bar that night, with Dad. But how could those boys have found John up here by the river, even if they'd been looking for him? No one has been able to find those kids anyway, not even Dad.

Walter was being so kind to her, but there was something different about him. And she knew him. At least, she thought she did. Better than most. Better than she had before she started dating him. She knew what he was capable of, and how he let his own needs warp the way he looked at things. And there was something different about him now.

Something made her turn left at the road. Away from her house. Toward Walter's house. She looked as she walked, but she didn't know why. *What am I looking for?*

She was about halfway to Walter's house when she saw it. Something glinted in the ditch at the side of the road, like metal. It had rained hard last night and the ground was wet, the blades of grass bending with the weight of the water. Curious, she walked toward it. Kneeling down, she reached into the muddy grass. Her hand touched something hard, and she pulled it out.

A hammer! Is that blood?

"Oh, no!" said Smith. He put the book down and frowned.

This is ridiculous! I don't believe it. What's going on?

Chapter 8

Marie turned right at the road and walked into town. This isn't what she had in mind for her honeymoon, but she had enough instincts of her own to respect Jeremy's. She knew it had to be done.

Once in town, the cell phone still didn't work. Marie found the bookstore easily. As she walked in, she was greeted by the young man behind the counter.

"Hi, can I help you?"

"Hi, Tony isn't it? I'm Marie Smith, a friend of the Lynne's."

"Oh, Jeremy's bride! Welcome. Have you started that book yet?"

Marie smiled. "Not yet. Actually, I was wondering if I could use your phone for a local call. I need to find Bob Penny and my cell phone doesn't work."

"Yeah, service is very spotty up here. We really need another tower. Is everything okay?"

"Yes, but it *is* important."

"No problem." Tony looked at his watch. "He could be at the barracks now. I'll dial for you."

He punched in a number and handed Marie the phone.

"Bob Penny here."

"Hello, Bob, this is Marie Smith, Jeremy Smith's wife."

"Oh, hello Marie. What can I do for you? Maggie and I are looking forward to seeing you two at the wedding tomorrow."

"Well, I wonder if you'd mind seeing us a little sooner. Jeremy sent me to town to call you because our cell phone wasn't working, but we found something you need to see. He stayed there."

"Where are you?"

"I'm at the bookstore."

"I'll be right there."

Marie handed the phone back to Tony.

"Is this something to do with Jason Berger's death?" he asked. "That was a waste."

"I'm not sure, actually. So anyway, I do plan to start reading that book today."

"Hey, you know, Richard—the author—he's in town. I saw him today. Maybe he can sign it for you. Oh, wait, he's Jason's cousin. That must be why he's here."

That's interesting, thought Marie. *I'll have to remember to tell Jeremy.* "Then maybe it's not the best time to ask him to sign a book."

"You're right about that."

The bell over the door tinkled, and Marie turned back to look.

"Well, here I am," said a tall, muscular, blonde young man in slacks and a button-down shirt. "You must be Marie."

"Hi, Bob," said Marie, holding out her hand. "It's nice to meet you. Jeremy said such nice things about you. Thank you so much for coming."

"No problem," said Penny, shaking her hand. "Let's get going."

Marie turned back toward Tony. "Thanks. I guess I'll see you again soon."

"Right. Tomorrow afternoon. See you then."

Penny held the door to the patrol car open for Marie, then he went around to the driver's side and slid behind the wheel. He turned to Marie. "Now, what's this about?"

"We did a canoe trip down the river, and ended up at that place just above the falls. Right outside of town, you know?"

Penny nodded his head.

"Anyway, we looked around a little before calling for our ride back to the RV park, and Jeremy ... well, we were just about to call when he saw something. There's a hammer in the grass alongside the path, and he thinks it may have blood on it and human hair. Do you know what color hair Jason Berger had, by any chance?"

"Brown."

"This was brown. Jeremy didn't want to leave the spot, so when our cell phone wouldn't work, he sent me to town to try to find you."

Penny shook his head. "I don't know how we could have missed something like that. I responded personally to the dispatcher's call on this one. I was already in town at the time, so I was the closest. The entire area was searched, I know it was. But we'd better get over there and see what we can see."

It took just two minutes to drive to the parking area. Marie led Penny over to where Smith waited. They both looked surprised at Smith's first words.

"This doesn't make sense!"

"What doesn't make sense?" asked Marie.

"This book." He held up the book. "There's a hammer with blood and hair in this book also."

"You're kidding," said Marie.

"No, but in the book, the hammer isn't found so close to the murder site. The girl finds it later, on the side of the road in a ditch."

"You're right," said Penny. "Something strange is going on here. Can I see the hammer?"

Smith parted the grass with the pen and pointed it out. Penny pulled out a pair of gloves and an evidence bag and reached for it.

"No, I don't know how we could have missed this. It's not possible." Penny studied the head of the hammer very closely before placing it in the bag.

"Oh," said Marie, "I almost forgot. Tony mentioned that the book's author's in town. He's actually related to the boy who died."

"Stranger and stranger," said Smith.

"Now, that's interesting," said Penny. "Yes, I discovered that already. Richard Tomlinson is Jason's cousin. But I didn't know he was here. He must have come down from Boston to be with his aunt. He doesn't have any other family in town. I wonder just when it was he got here. I was told he once had a crush on Beth himself. Say, Jeremy, how would you feel about coming with me to talk to them right now?"

Marie sighed as she looked into Jeremy's eager yet concerned eyes. Penny noticed their silent communication.

"Look, it's your honeymoon. I—"

"No," said Marie, "this is important. I understand. But what about me and the canoe?"

"No problem," said Penny "Let's go over to my car. I'll radio Jimmy to bring the pickup here."

"Jimmy?" said Marie.

"Jimmy Benson. He's one of the state troopers at the satellite station. I'm the investigator assigned to this satellite by the Bureau."

"Bureau?" said Smith.

"Bureau of Criminal Investigation. State police. So then, we'll get you and the canoe safely back to that RV park before we go. It's right on the way."

"Oh, it is, is it?" said Marie with a sour look on her face. "I guess that's lucky for me."

The two men looked at her with surprise and concern. Marie started to laugh. The men joined her, though cautiously at first.

"Just kidding," she said. "Let's get me and the canoe settled, and then you guys go and do your thing. Dinner'll only take half an hour tonight, Jeremy, so I'll start it when you get back. If you'll be later than six-thirty, can you call me?"

"Will do."

"Meantime, I plan to start reading that book!"

Chapter 9

Penny made a right turn off the main road and onto a smaller road that was barely wider than a driveway. Smith read the street sign as they turned—Marshy Lane. Sure enough, as they drove, the land on their left opened up to what looked like wetlands, with a stream running through. *This is the wettest place*, thought Smith. *Streams and ponds and lakes everywhere you go.*

After about five minutes, the ground seemed to dry up. They passed a group of wild turkeys, two deer, and many squirrels and chipmunks. A very fat and surprisingly fast woodchuck ran across the road in front of the car. An occasional bird also flew right in front of them. Smith wondered if they were suicidal or just the daredevils of the family.

Finally, they drove up to an old farmhouse on the right. There were several cows behind a fence, and a barn with a red silo. In the distance, Smith saw a very large, plowed field. Penny pulled into the driveway and parked in front of a second, smaller barn-like structure, about a hundred feet before the house. He beeped his horn twice and got out. Smith followed.

The door to the farmhouse opened, and a young man came out. He looked to be a little younger than Penny, with dark brown, collar-length hair and a sharp, angular face. He was short—about Smith's height—but as narrow as Smith was broad.

"Richard," said Penny, "when did you get here?"

"Aunt Kathy called me as soon ... as soon as ..." Richard paused and took a deep breath. "Well, anyway, I came right away. Have you found out anything?" Richard glanced over at Smith, and then back at Penny with a question in his eyes.

"This is Jeremy Smith," said Penny "He's a friend of Jenny Lynne's family, here for the wedding."

Richard nodded. "Well, come on in. Aunt Kathy's inside, but she isn't much up to talking. Between dealing with all this and trying to figure out how to run this farm alone, she's just about all used up."

"Any chance you'll be moving back here?"

"Please, Bob, don't say that inside. I feel terrible about Jason, but I'm staying in Boston. Aunt Kathy will have to hire someone to manage it, or else sell, I guess."

Smith had listened to this exchange carefully. He hadn't heard anything suspicious yet. He followed the other two men into the house. They passed through a small living area and then directly into the kitchen—no doorway separated the rooms. It was an old kitchen, and unlike Barbara and Allan's, it felt like one. Although it was a tidy room, the appliances were old and worn, the floor was linoleum with the edges curling up, and the room needed painting. Even the kitchen table was chipped, and one leg was badly repaired. It was here that another small, angular person sat—a woman with reddened eyes. She looked to be a little older than Smith.

"Hello, Mrs. Berger," said Penny.

The woman looked up at them with a blank stare.

"I'm sorry to bother you again so soon. This is Jeremy Smith, a friend of the Lynne's, up for the wedding. He was in town when Jason was found after his ... accident, and he's found something up near the falls that may or may not mean anything—"

"I knew it!" The blank face came alive. "It wasn't an accident! I thought about it, Bob. It's Arthur! I know it! He killed my boy. He couldn't stand it that Beth left him for my Jason, and he killed him! He killed him, he killed him, he killed him …"

Kathy Berger broke into tears, and her voice became softer and softer, the words coming out, now, as automatically as her breath.

Her nephew went up to her and patted her back. "Aunt Kathy, please stop saying that. There's no reason to think it. Please, I'm worried about you."

"Mrs. Berger," said Penny, gently, "is there any reason for you to think that Arthur would actually want to hurt Jason? I mean, have they had any arguments that you know about or anything."

She took a deep breath. "I know he didn't like Jason going out with Beth. I could see it in his face when they ran into each other in town."

"I'm wondering," said Penny, turning toward Richard, "Jeremy, here, started to read your book, and it seems like there are some similarities between the book and this situation. You know how some people in town didn't like you writing it because it was too much like Jack Hunter and Gwendolyn—"

"But it's nothing like that! My book is completely fiction. I don't even give the characters any similar traits to Hunter and Gwen. There's nothing in Hunter's history to even suggest that his death was a murder. It just gave me an idea for the backdrop of the story. There's nothing the same between my characters and those two. But these people around here haven't even read it to see for themselves."

Smith stepped forward. "But there do seem to be quite a lot of similarities between your book and what's happened here, now—today. Do you know Beth White?"

Richard looked startled when Smith spoke up, but Smith saw only confusion at his question.

"Yes, of course. We were all in the same class together—me, Beth, and Arthur. Jason was two years ahead."

"Were you close?"

Richard hesitated. "When we were younger, maybe. By high school, Beth and Arthur only had time for each other, pretty much."

"Do you know if Arthur read your book?"

"Yes. He did—one of the few. He wrote me about it, actually. He liked it. But I don't understand. It's just a book. I wrote it before they broke up, and I never thought they would. And I'd have no way of knowing she'd start seeing Jason. What are you getting at? Do you think Arthur got the idea to break up with Beth from my book or something? That doesn't make sense. And why are *you* asking me questions anyway?"

Penny spoke up. "Jeremy's a homicide detective. He's helping me out."

"Homicide detective! But ... What *did* you find out there, anyway?"

Neither Penny nor Smith answered, but Smith saw a light come on in Richard's eyes. "Wait, no way! That's crazy! Is it possible that Arthur ... No, it can't be."

"Why not?" shouted his aunt. "They've found something!"

"We're not sure we've found anything important yet," said Penny. "We still have to determine that. We'll let you know as soon as we do. Anyway, I guess you'll be around for a few days at least, then, Richard?"

"Yes, at least a week or two."

"When can I have Jason back?" said Mrs. Berger. "We need to make the plans."

"It'll just be a day or two more," said Penny. "I'll let you know later today. So, okay then, I'll be in touch."

Richard stayed with his aunt, who had begun to cry again, and waved apologetically. Smith followed Penny out.

"Well," said Smith, as soon as they got into the patrol car, "he didn't seem to be at all uncomfortable when I brought up the similarity between his book and Jason's death."

"No, I saw that," said Penny. "I'm glad we planned it that *you* brought that up. I wasn't looking forward to it, and it was a good idea to try to catch him off guard. But he *didn't* let on how much he liked Beth in high school, at least according to the gossip I've heard around town."

"Yes, I saw that too. But even though his aunt seems to be convinced that Arthur killed Jason, Richard didn't try to support that belief, at least not at first."

Penny rubbed his chin with his left hand. "Well, you know, if Jason and Arthur got into a fight or something, that might have made more sense. But if what we're looking at here—if it's anything at all—turns out to be something planned …" Penny shook his head. "No, that's not consistent with Arthur's character. And, did you notice, Richard talked about Arthur breaking up with Beth. I had heard it was Beth that did the breaking up."

"Barbara told me that *Beth* did the breaking up but it was because *Arthur* didn't want to make a commitment. So I guess our next stop is the right one to make. And it's very convenient that Arthur's at Beth's house."

"He was there when I called Beth, anyway, and I asked them both to stay until we got there."

"Okay, then. So, let's go see if a sudden question from a stranger has any more effect there than it did here!"

Chapter 10

Beth lived in town with her parents, which was about a ten-minute drive. They were almost there when Penny got a call on the radio from Jimmy.

"Bob, it *is* blood on the hammer, and human hair. The DNA will take a few days, but we'll get the blood type today. And we have prints on the hammer."

"Hey, now, Jimmy, *that's* surprising, but good to hear. We need to get prints to compare. I want everyone's who knew Jason, if we can get'em. I know I should want to solve this case, but I'm sort of hoping that we can rule everyone out and call it a chance encounter with a violent stranger."

"We have some people's prints already, on file—I know that some of Jason's friends provided them to the department in their youth."

Smith, listening to the conversation, laughed at this suggestion of youthful hijinks. Penny looked over at him with an answering smile.

"That's good, Jimmy. Get started with those, and we'll see where we want to go from there. Call me immediately if you get a hit. I'm just pulling into town now. I'll be at Beth White's house. I guess I'll leave my phone on. Use my cell."

"Right."

Penny replaced the mouthpiece.

"I thought cell phones don't work around here," said Smith.

Penny smiled. "They don't work everywhere. It's very spotty. Annoying, isn't it? But local emergency services have a small tower with a private frequency. Our phones will work almost everywhere—though there are some blackout areas, even for us, because of all the trees and the mountains."

"I was listening to what you were just saying," said Smith, "and it *is* a surprise that there are prints on that hammer. I can't imagine someone intentionally leaving that hammer there without wiping it clean. Someone must have been in a hurry to get out of there—maybe it dropped out of their pocket or something, and they didn't notice until it was too late."

"That would make it seem like an unplanned murder, though, and why would someone bring a hammer to a meeting in the woods without a plan? Of course, it could've been that stranger I was hoping for that Jason ran afoul of."

"*If* the hammer even has anything to do with Jason's death," said Smith. "We're not really sure about that yet."

"We'll know that soon enough, anyway."

"And if someone had a tool kit with them or something, there could have been a hammer there without a murder plan."

"True."

Penny had driven past the falls on the right, past the left turn that went toward the Lynne's house, and straight onto Main Street. At the end of the three blocks of shops, to Smith's right, was a bridge that crossed the river into Pennsylvania. Penny turned left.

They passed mostly private homes on small lots for about two blocks. Then the area opened up again and had more of a rural feel, and the houses and lots were larger.

After two more blocks, Penny turned right into the driveway of what looked to Smith like a Craftsmen-style house—he thought they called it Arts and Crafts style in the Northeast. The siding was made of dark brown shingles, and the trim and lattice were white. It was a nice-sized house—Smith guessed it to be about 2400 square feet.

"What are those shingles made of, do you know?" asked Smith.

"That's cedar."

"I thought so," said Smith.

The two men walked up onto the front porch and rang the bell. The front door was already open, and through the screen, Smith saw a young woman approach.

She was of average height and weight—he guessed about 5 feet 4 inches, 120 pounds—and had short, wavy black hair. She wasn't beautiful, but she was close to it. Smith figured that if she wore makeup, the adjective would fit. He also thought that, with her large eyes and freckles, she looked very much like Marie must have had looked when she was her age. It made him feel very fatherly toward the girl. Acknowledging this feeling, Smith recognized that it could influence his reactions and interpretations, and he made a mental note to be alert for that.

When Beth reached the door, the sunlight hit her face, and Smith could see that she had been crying.

"Hello, Beth," said Penny. "I'm sorry to bother you now. I know you've lost a friend."

"Hi, Bob. Come on in."

The men entered and followed Beth as she led them through a hallway that sported a beautiful, old wooden floor. The staircase on the right was built with the same deep, rich-colored wood—the stairs and the banister both. A burgundy runner on the staircase echoed the one on the hallway floor. Passing out of the hallway, they entered a stunning dining room, which had, in addition to the wood floors, some amazing wood moldings, both baseboard and window moldings, as well as a built-in, wooden cupboard on the left, across from the windows.

Straight ahead, an archway separated the dining room from the living room, where the moldings and wood floor continued, and where a young man sat waiting on the couch. He stood up as they approached.

"Hi, Arthur," said Penny. "Thanks for hanging around here for me."

The two men shook hands.

"So, who's this?" asked Arthur. "Where's Jimmy?"

"This is Jeremy Smith. He's a friend of the Lynne's, here for Jenny's wedding, and he happens to be a very experienced detective from San Francisco. He's helping me out."

"Why do you need help," asked Beth. "Wasn't it an accident? I was hoping …"

"What do you mean, 'hoping?'" asked Penny. "I was wanting to ask you anyway, since you were dating Jason, if you knew anything that we should know that could help us to sort out this tragedy."

"No, I wasn't. I mean, I wasn't dating him anymore. That's why … I mean, we just broke up a few weeks ago. Arthur …"

She looked over at Arthur, who took up the tale. "I realized what a fool I had been to let the person who was the other half of me get away. That's what Beth's trying to say." He walked over to Beth and took her hand.

Smith was as surprised as Penny was, judging by the expression on Penny's face. This definitely took away one motive. *I wonder if that's the idea*, Smith thought. *Are they making this up?* He decided to jump in here and see how the pair reacted.

"How did *Jason* feel about this?"

Again, Smith was surprised. He expected to see defensiveness, or anger, or annoyance. Maybe even guilt—not necessarily the kind that would be an admission of anything, but just the human response of guilt from having your actions cause pain, even if there was nothing wrong with what you did. Instead, looking closely at Arthur's face as he asked this question, and into his eyes, Smith saw only sadness, the sincerity of which was mirrored in Beth's eyes.

"He was devastated," said Beth. "I ... I started seeing him in good faith. He told me how much he had always cared for me and respected me, and what a fool Arthur was to not understand what was important in life. I needed to hear things like that, I guess. But also, I really believed that it was over between me and Arthur. He ... I broke up with him, technically, but he had made it clear ..."

"I made it clear that I needed to sow my wild oats and see what else was out there in the world. I didn't give her any other choice really. I wanted to make her be the one to do it, so I wouldn't have to. I knew how much she wanted to share her life with me, plan a family, the whole thing. I'm not usually a coward, and I'm not sure I was being one here. I wanted her to have that control—to not feel like a victim. I didn't realize how this one mistake I made could end up with Jason being hurt so badly."

"I didn't break up with Jason because of Arthur," continued Beth, "but he still was so upset. That's what I meant by 'hoping,'" said Beth. "I was hoping that it wasn't what I thought—that he hadn't done something stupid."

"What do you mean?" asked Penny.

"I was worried about him," said Beth. "He'd been so upset, I thought he might not watch what he was doing, or might have tried to go over the falls on purpose—like a macho thing, for his bruised ego, or something. Actually, I went over to his Mom's yesterday morning and told her I was worried about how he was acting since we broke up. But maybe it was to late."

This time, Smith noted that there was no reaction on Penny's face, but he had to be feeling as stunned as Smith did on the inside.

"So," said Penny, casually, "you saw Mrs. Berger yesterday?"

"Yes. Didn't she mention it? I would have thought she'd have told you, given ... given what happened."

"No, she didn't," said Penny, "but she's pretty much in shock. So, Mrs. Berger knew, then, that you broke up with Jason?"

"Oh, yes. I explained it to her. And she also knew it wasn't because Arthur wanted me back. After about three or four weeks of dating, Jason seemed to change. He wanted to know where I was every minute. He was very demanding. I needed to end it anyway. I had already talked to Mrs. Berger before about some of that—about how he was acting. But it's still very sad. He was a good person, really. He just was in a lot of pain. I think it was still from his father's death, you know. He hid it well from everyone, but inside, when I got closer to him, I could see a little boy who never recovered from it."

"I see," said Penny. "Well, that was very helpful. It gives us something else to think about. I appreciate it. So, now, it's just routine, but Arthur, where were you yesterday afternoon?"

"I was home."

"Alone?"

"Yes, after lunch, anyway. I had lunch there with my mom before she went in to the store."

"And you, Beth?"

"I went into the city. I had some shopping to do. I went straight after talking to Kathy—to Mrs. Berger."

"Also alone?"

She looked over at Arthur. "Yes."

Smith noted a surprised look on Arthur's face. "Alone? But—"

Beth glanced at Arthur again and sighed. "Oh, well, then. I told Arthur that I was meeting a girlfriend in the city for lunch and shopping, but I was really getting him a birthday present. I have a receipt from Sporting Way."

"Beth!"

"It's not a lie, you know, when it's for something loving!"

"Would you mind if I took a look at that receipt?" asked Penny.

52

Beth left the room, and was back in a minute. She handed a store receipt to Penny. He looked closely at it.

"Okay, then, it has the time printed on it and everything. Will you both be around for the next few days? Not going anywhere?"

"No," said Arthur, "we'll be here."

"Good, that's all for now, then."

"Bob," said Beth, "I was thinking of going to see Mrs. Berger, to comfort her, but …"

"No," said Penny, "I'd hold off on that for awhile, Beth. I don't think she's ready to see you yet."

"Oh," said Beth, looking into Bob's eyes. "I see. I understand."

"Good. Then, we'll be going now. We'll keep in touch with both of you."

Beth walked Penny and Smith to the door. They said a final goodbye and got into the patrol car. Penny held his hand up, stopping Smith before he spoke. He drove off down the road toward town, pulled off into an empty field, and turned off the engine.

"Okay, now," said Penny. "What do you make of that?"

"Well, a lot. My first thought was she might be trying to take away Arthur's motive by claiming they were back together. But it was so intricate and spontaneous—their account, I mean. Then I thought that, maybe, if it's true that they were back together, Jason might have challenged one or both if them, and they might have needed to defend themselves. I think both ideas are still possible. Neither of them have a perfect alibi—not even Beth. You'd need to make sure she was the one who was at the store getting that receipt. Another thing—Beth stopped short of saying she thought Jason might have committed suicide, but the suicide possibility would explain the shoes found on the bank—"

"Yes, that's true!"

"But it wouldn't explain the hammer," continued Smith. "Unless there's someone else involved that we don't know about. Still, we haven't tied the hammer to Jason's death yet, and you didn't find it there yesterday."

"It's very strange that Jason's mom didn't mention Beth's visit yesterday morning. What I said about her being in shock is true, but still …"

"Yeah, 'but still.' And I don't think Richard knew that Beth and Jason had broken up, or he would have mentioned it when his aunt was going on about Arthur. Still, based on how I'm reading Beth and Arthur, I would still be leaning toward an accident, or even suicide, if it weren't for that darn—"

Penny's cell phone rang. Smith nodded and waved his hand at it.

"Yep," said Penny, before answering. "That darn hammer!" He pressed a button and put the phone to his ear. "Penny here. Yes, Jimmy, what do you have?" Smith watched as Penny's face fell. "I see. Yes. Okay then. No, I'll do it. We'll be in soon."

He hung up and turned to Smith.

"What is it?" asked Smith.

"The prints on the hammer are Arthur's."

"No! You're kidding! Why do you have Arthur's prints? I guess he isn't the angel everyone is making out."

"It's nothing like that. Apparently, in Junior High, he joined a junior firefighters group. One of the things the group did was put their fingerprints on file."

"Why?"

"It beats me, but we would have taken them now anyway if we needed to. Anyway, the blood is the same blood type as Jason's. The DNA on the hair and the blood will take a while, but it's enough for now. I have to arrest him. Do you mind staying with me until I get him to Mountlake? I'd like to pick him up now and take him straight there. It's a thirty or forty minute drive, but then I can introduce you to my supervisor there, also."

"No problem. I guess I'll call Marie and tell her it'll be another, what, hour and a half or so?"

"Yeah. When we get him in, I'll have someone drive you right back."

"Okay, then, but Beth said something that I thought was interesting, and I wanted to make sure you caught it."

"What?"

"Before she went to get the receipt, she said something like, 'It isn't lying when it's done for love.'"

Chapter 11

"I don't understand," said Arthur.

"We need to bring you to the Bureau of Criminal Investigation in Mountlake, Arthur," said Penny, for the second time.

"But you've just read me my rights! You're serious, then. What's going on?"

"I'm sorry about this. I really am. But you're under arrest for the murder of Jason Berger. And I hope you *heard* what I told you about your rights. Did you understand them? Do you have an attorney you want to call?"

"What? No, of course not. I don't need an attorney. This doesn't make sense. Look, let's just go, then, and I'm sure we can straighten this all out. There must be some mistake. We'll clear it all up."

"Of course it's a mistake!" said Beth. She heard her own voice as if it were someone else's. Even in her disbelief and shock, she realized that the calmness of her voice was based more on numbness than on maturity. "Bob, you *know* Arthur couldn't do something like that."

"I'm sorry, Beth. Arthur, I have to take you in."

Beth looked at Bob and at the policeman friend of the Lynne's, but she couldn't look at Arthur, even though she felt his gaze on her.

"Beth?" Arthur said, confusion in his voice.

Beth sighed, realizing she had to find the strength somehow—that she couldn't let go yet. She looked up at Arthur, and tears filled her eyes. She stood up and went to him, burying her head in his shoulder and smelling his scent as if it was the last time she might ever see him.

"Don't worry," said Arthur, his lips in her hair, "it'll be okay."

After the three men left, Beth got up and went into her bedroom. She closed the door and pulled the shades down, as if trying to shut out the world—and the truth of what had just happened. At first, when they left, she had felt as though she couldn't breath—as though she might die. Now, she felt her heart close off from the world, like a door slamming, and the pain lessened.

In her room, she could think. Outside her room, the world threatened to push its way back in again, and the effort of keeping it out precluded clear thought. It didn't seem fair, somehow. She had already dealt with the pain of life without Arthur once. To have to do it again so soon—no, it was unthinkable. She wouldn't allow it.

What was it that Bob asked—where was Arthur yesterday afternoon? And Arthur had said, "Home. Alone."

Why didn't they ask me first? I would have said we were together. I would do anything to keep us together now. I wouldn't give up so easily this time. Why didn't Arthur think of that—realize why they were asking and know he had to say he wasn't alone? The library was closed yesterday, so I was off. It would have made sense that Arthur would take a little time off from the market to be with me. But it was too late now.

Of course, *she* knew he didn't do it—kill Jason. That wasn't the point. It was ridiculous that anyone thought he could have done that. But how could she possibly prove it? What evidence could they have found that Jason was murdered, let alone that made them think it was Arthur who did it?

Beth heard her mother come home. "Beth," her mom called out. She didn't answer. Beth knew her father was right behind. He had picked up her mother after work on his way home from a sales meeting in Scranton.

It was late, and Beth was supposed to have made dinner tonight. She guessed they would understand when they found out. But that meant she would have to tell them. She would have to say the words out loud. And that was something she was going to put off for as long as she could.

Chapter 12

It only took half an hour to get to the office in Mountlake. The two-story building housed the central office for the state police in this district. After leaving Arthur in an interrogation room with a uniformed trooper, Penny took Smith down a long hall, windowless and lit with fluorescent light, to meet his supervisor. They were buzzed into an office by another uniformed trooper. Smith was surprised at the natural light that flooded the room, in contrast to the hallway.

Senior Investigator Marc Jacobs looked up from the report he was reading. He ran his hand over his closely cropped, graying hair, wrinkled his forehead, and yawned.

"Sorry, it's been a long day. So, is this Inspector Smith?"

Smith didn't even notice that Jacobs called him by a title he didn't have any more. It still seemed natural to him.

"Yes," said Penny. "Jeremy Smith, this is Senior Investigator Jacobs."

"Call me Marc. So, you decided to get yourself a busman's holiday, I see."

Smith smiled. "I don't want to butt in—"

"Not at all," said Jacobs. "We appreciate your help. I'm hoping we won't need any more of it though." Jacobs looked pointedly at Penny, who kept his face impassive. "And I hope you get to enjoy the rest of your stay here. Although, I did take the time to call San Francisco when Investigator Penny first told me you were coming—I met your Captain Harris at a convention in Denver a few years back, and we've stayed in touch."

Smith smiled. "He's a good cop. He was my lieutenant before he was promoted."

"So I hear. And it seems that, according to him, you've got quite a reputation there. So, if any thoughts come to you while you're here, don't hesitate to share them. You won't be stepping on anyone's toes, I don't think." He looked over at Penny.

"No, of course not," said Penny.

"Well," said Smith, "if I can help, I will."

Jacobs held out his hand. "It was nice meeting you, Inspector Smith."

"Yes, same here," said Smith, shaking his hand. "And it's Jeremy."

Jacobs turned to Penny. "Investigator Penny, after you show Inspector Smith out, come back. I want to discuss the interrogation before you go in with Walker."

"Right."

The two men turned and left the office. Smith looked at Penny quizzically.

Penny smiled. "It's okay. I'd talk the same way to someone else in the same situation. Missing that hammer! Anyway, Jacobs is a good guy. And he doesn't say things he doesn't mean. If you have any thoughts on this, feel free to share them."

"You *know* what I think. The coincidence with the book bothers me. And your not finding that hammer doesn't make sense. On the other hand, you can't ignore the evidence. And Arthur *did* read that book, according to Richard. You just have to do your thing. This is one of those one-step-at-a-time kinds of cases I think. And your next step, I guess, is seeing what Arthur says. Do you want me to listen in on your interrogation?"

"No, you've helped enough. Too much, I'm thinking. Go back to your honeymoon, Jeremy. Neither one of us likes this outcome, but it has to be done. Let's get you that ride back home."

Smith hid his disappointment. "Right. Good luck, then."

*****

"I still don't understand how you could think I did something like that," said Arthur, quietly and calmly. "I know there must be some mistake. You're absolutely sure someone killed Jason?"

Bob Penny was looking closely at Arthur as he spoke. He had to admit that his calmness didn't seem forced, or in any way like he was using it to hide something, although Penny could sense a little bit of confusion underlying it. Arthur looked out of place in this room, sitting on an old wooden chair at the bare wooden table.

Penny almost wished Arthur *had* insisted on a lawyer before talking to him—he didn't seem to understand yet that he needed one. But even if Jacobs hadn't been behind that mirror, listening in on the interrogation, Penny wasn't about to suggest it now. He had already read him his rights, as Arthur had put it.

"We're pretty sure of that," Penny answered, finally, "or we wouldn't have brought you in."

"But even so, why would you think *I* would do something like that? We didn't grow up together, Bob, but you know me. I can see how, maybe, the thought would cross your mind because Beth and I broke up, but now that you know we're back together ... I don't understand. And even if Beth and I were still apart, I wouldn't ever think of hurting someone—you know that. You must!"

"I know that people—even the best of people—can find themselves in a situation where they do things they never thought they would do."

"But why? Can't you tell me why you think I did this?"

Penny sighed. "You're sure you were alone at home? No one saw you or spoke to you?"

"Yes, I'm sure."

"Why weren't you at work?"

"I don't have to be at the market every minute. You know what a good group of employees we have. I often take Thursday off because that's Beth's day off, but she had those other plans yesterday. People don't usually think they have to have alibis, Bob." Arthur paused. "You're not thinking *Beth* had anything to do with this, are you?"

"No." Penny hesitated, then walked over to a side counter and picked up a plastic bag. He walked back to the table, dropped the bag down in front of Arthur, and watched him very closely.

Arthur looked at it and frowned. "A hammer? Is that what you think happened? Someone hit him with this? Oh, God, I can see there's blood on it. And is that hair?"

Again, Penny didn't see Arthur holding anything back. His surprise had seemed sincere. His concern—even disgust—had seemed sincere. And Arthur had looked him right in the eye. Unless he was a lifelong sociopath and no one in town had figured that out yet, how could he possibly seem so ... so innocent!

But the facts were there. And maybe there *was* more to Arthur than many people realized. After all, everyone says that Beth was the one who broke it off, even if she and Arthur are saying now that he purposely drove her to it, and even if Barbara Lynne said the same thing. But maybe there was some other reason she wanted to end the relationship— something about Arthur.

And there was Jason's mom. She seemed to think Arthur was capable of this. If Beth had told the truth about telling Mrs. Berger she had broken up with Jason, Mrs.

Berger would know that Arthur wouldn't have much of a motive. So why would she still think Arthur did this unless she knew something more about him or his personality?

Or maybe something *did* happen to provoke Arthur, like maybe Jason attacked Arthur or Beth, and Arthur fought back. If these two were protecting each other, they might be motivated enough to tap into some pretty good acting skills. Any old way Penny looked at it, he couldn't get past the evidence. It was time to confront Arthur.

"Arthur," he said quietly, "the hammer has your fingerprints on it."

"What?"

Again, there wasn't even the slightest hesitation before Arthur's face showed confusion, this time followed, for the first time, by a real look of concern. Arthur peered down at the hammer.

"Can I turn the package over?"

"Let me do it," said Penny.

Again, Arthur peered down at it. "Oh, my God! It's my hammer. Look at that chip, and the paint on the side of the handle. Oh, my God, I don't understand."

"So, you can see that we have a problem here, Arthur. Do you have any explanation?"

Arthur was quiet for a minute. Penny could see him thinking.

"I don't understand this, but either someone coincidentally used my hammer to kill Jason, or else someone used it on purpose to make it look like I did it. Either way, I think I *will* be needing to talk to a lawyer, Investigator Penny."

Chapter 13

Something still didn't sit right with Smith. He sat across from Marie, mechanically eating his dinner in silence.

"Are you okay?" asked Marie.

Smith almost jumped. "Oh! Yes, I'm fine. Sorry. I guess I've been somewhere else."

"Is it this case?"

Smith sighed. "I know it's not my business, but something isn't right—"

The phone rang. Smith got up and answered it, grateful that the RV park was one of those spots that had cell phone service.

"Hello?"

"Hi, Jeremy, it's Bob."

"Oh, hi! What's up?"

"I just finished talking with Arthur."

There was a moment of silence.

"And ..." said Smith.

"And, unless he's a great actor or a sociopath, I would normally be inclined to think he was innocent—if the evidence wasn't so clear. We still don't have DNA, but the hair on the hammer looks like a match for Jason's. I have no choice but to hold him."

"Did he have any explanation for the hammer being there? I mean, maybe he handled one of Jason's hammers a while ago and Jason had it with him, and maybe some third party used it as a weapon of convenience, unplanned."

"Hey, that's a good scenario, but no, he was completely mystified by it. Oh, and it's not just the prints. He identified it as being his hammer because of a chip on it and some paint."

"Oh."

"That's when he asked for a lawyer—the fingerprints and it being his hammer. He wasn't at all fazed by the hammer alone when I dropped it down in front of him. But when he knew it was his, he said someone must be trying to frame him on purpose."

"It could be. If someone didn't know Jason and Beth broke up, he'd be a good patsy."

"It didn't seem like Richard knew," said Penny, hesitantly.

"No, it didn't. But there could be someone else who had a beef with Jason—an employee, a friend, a customer. Maybe he overcharged someone or messed up an order."

"All that's possible, I know," said Penny. "But also, maybe it was Jason that attacked Arthur or Beth, and Arthur defended himself or her, and the two of them worked out their innocent act together. Or maybe Arthur couldn't get past his jealousy, even if he and Beth *were* back together. Or maybe they weren't really back together—Mrs. Berger didn't seem to know it, even though Beth says she told her. Maybe this is all about protecting Arthur."

Smith sighed. "That's not our gut feeling, though, is it?"

"No, it's not." Penny paused. "We'll do a little more work on our end, looking for another possible suspect. I'll definitely talk to Richard tomorrow. But that's all I can do. I have to hold Arthur."

"I know. I'm not sure what's more frustrating in police work—knowing someone did it and not being able to prove it, or feeling like they might be innocent and having to go with the evidence."

"Tell me about it! Anyway, say hello to Marie for me. I'll let you know if something comes up tomorrow. Otherwise, I'll see you later in the day, at the wedding."

"Looking forward to it. And looking forward to meeting Maggie. Bye."

"Bye."

Smith hit "end" on the cell phone, pushed away the plate that held his mostly-finished dinner, and looked up at Marie.

"I heard your part," she said. "I guess you really didn't think he did it."

"No, I guess I didn't. Or else, I just didn't *want* to think it. I thought it was a great idea I had, that Arthur had handled a hammer of Jason's, and it could have let Arthur off the hook if he hadn't admitted the hammer was his."

"So why did he admit it?"

"I guess because it's true. And that's one reason I still wonder if he did it, despite the evidence." Smith hesitated before sharing his next thought. "Actually, I'm supposed to remind myself of something." He paused.

"What?"

"It's about Beth—Arthur's girlfriend, who dated Jason for a month or two?"

Marie nodded.

"Beth kind of looks like you looked when you were her age. It's almost like she could be our daughter. It makes me feel fatherly toward her, and I'm wondering if I'm letting that influence my judgment."

Marie started to laugh, then held it back. "You don't usually let emotion cloud your thinking," she said, solemnly. "Any anyway, didn't I hear you say that Bob Penny has the same feeling—that maybe Arthur didn't do it?"

"Yes, that's true." Smith decided to ignore Marie's almost-laugh. "But Bob also mentioned other scenarios where he might have done it—in self defense, if Jason was the attacker, or else, maybe Beth and Jason didn't break up, but she's protecting Arthur now."

"But if Beth and Jason didn't break up, why would Beth *want* to cover for Arthur?"

"She could still love Arthur." Smith shook his head. "I wish I could talk to people who knew them all, to get a better picture of things. Then, maybe I would know."

Smith could see that Marie was thinking hard about something. "Well," she said, finally, "the library is open tomorrow. I don't know if Beth will be there, but her co-workers will. And I'd bet that people who work in a library would know most of the people in this town."

Smith smiled. He leaned across the dinette table, took Marie's face in his hands, and planted a big kiss on her lips. "You are brilliant, you know. I'm not even surprised."

This time, Marie did laugh out loud, that musical and infectious laugh that Smith loved so much. He couldn't help but join in.

"So," said Marie, "how about we clean up here and take the dogs for a nice walk."

"Okay," said Smith. "I'll dry."

Chapter 14

Smith was too wound up to go to sleep. After Marie kissed him goodnight, he picked up Richard's book one more time. The section he had read about the hammer was almost at the end, and he decided to continue reading from that point.

Turning off all but the small reading light above the sofa, he sat down and grabbed the book from the wicker storage cube that they used as both a coffee table and an extra seat. He could tell by the bookmark that was inside of it that Marie had finished more than half the book already. She was a fast reader. Careful not to lose her place, Smith found his own and began to read.

She was about halfway to Walter's house when she saw it. Something glinted in the ditch at the side of the road, like metal. It had rained hard last night and the ground was wet, the blades of grass bending with the weight of the water. Curious, she walked toward it. Kneeling down, she reached into the muddy grass. Her hand touched something hard, and she pulled it out.

A hammer! Is that blood?

Carolyn felt her heart start to pound. It felt as if it might break through her chest. Now that she found it, she didn't know what to do with it, or even if she should do anything.

It might not have anything to do with John's death. If it didn't and she brought it to the police, would it make them even less likely to listen to her than they were now? If this *were* evidence, would they even believe her? They didn't believe her about Walter. About how violent he could be. About how she was afraid of him. Good old Walter. They all thought she was some kind of emotional female who was still mad at him for breaking up with her. They didn't believe her that it was she who had pulled away from him—in fear. Well, what about good old John? *Her* John! Why didn't they want to make sure that *he* got justice?

Suddenly, Carolyn stiffened. Was that a rustling in the bushes? She brushed aside her fear, convincing herself that it must have been an animal or a bird. Then she heard it again. And this time she had the distinct feeling that she was being looked at— watched. She felt the hairs on the back of her neck stand up. The fear threatened to engulf her, but she didn't succumb. Taking a deep breath, she slowly stood up and turned around.

"Hello, Carolyn."

"Hello, Walter." Carolyn lowered her gaze briefly and scanned the area. There was nowhere to go—nowhere to run to. Casually, she inched her way into the center of the road as she looked back up at Walter. "What are you doing out here?"

"Funny. That's what I was going to ask you. With all your talk about murderers running around, I'm surprised you think it's safe to walk around by yourself."

Carolyn ignored this last comment. "Actually, I was on my way to see you. With everything you said to me about John, you had to know I would wonder—I'd have to. But the police are so sure it was an accident, and I …" Carolyn thought quickly. "I feel badly, now, about it. I was on my way to your house … to talk to you … to apologize."

"Were you now? Well, isn't that nice of you. You've always been such a *nice* girl, Carolyn. And smart. And you've got a good pair of eyes on you, I'll give you that. In fact, it seemed to me like you just found something over there that interested you."

Walter walked over to where Carolyn had been standing before and looked down. Carolyn saw *him* stiffen this time. Her heart sank.

"Well, well, well, little lady, it looks like you found the mother lode, now, didn't you. I bet you're proud of yourself, you little bitch."

If possible, Walter's voice had become even more unpleasant. She recognized the tone. She had heard it once before, when she broke up with him. She didn't see how she was going to get away this time. She opened her mouth to speak, but no words would come out. Suddenly, Walter pulled out a knife.

She turned and started to run, blindly, not knowing where, not hoping or thinking, a scream finally making its way out of her throat, past her lips. She felt a hand grab her arm. She fought against it—pulled against it—then turned, her hand raised in a fist. A hand grabbed her fist. She struggled.

"Carolyn."

She didn't hear her name, only a sound. Still, she struggled.

"Carolyn!" Louder this time. She stopped struggling and focused her eyes.

"Jed?" She felt the air rush back into her lungs. "Jed! Oh, Jed!" She collapsed into the officer's arms and started to cry, repeating, "Jed, Jed, Jed," through her sobs.

"It's okay now, little girl, it's okay." Jed patted the back of her head.

Finally, Carolyn straightened up. She looked over and saw Walter lying on the ground, unconscious. A young man she didn't recognize was kneeling by the ditch, picking up the hammer.

"What ... How ..."

"I kind of know you better than a lot of the boys, and I value your opinion. I brought the state in on it. We've been keeping an eye on Walter. We saw him walking out of town. Thought it strange—his car was right there. We followed him."

Carolyn looked back down at Walter. This time, she saw blood coming from his mouth. She was confused. "Is he ...?"

"He didn't drop the knife when I grabbed him," said Jed. "Didn't you hear the gun shot? My friend from the state, here, was right behind me."

The young man looked up at them. "It's definitely human hair and blood on the hammer. Peterson had blonde hair, didn't he?"

Carolyn sobbed.

"Yeah," said Jed. "That's right. Well, it looks like Walter saved us the expense of a trial." He looked down at Carolyn. "You're safe now, you know. You'll be okay. And John can rest in peace."

She looked up into his eyes. "Thank you, Jed. I know. But I won't be—not completely—until I'm with him again, with John. I've lost the other half of myself, and I know someday we'll be put back together again."

Smith closed the book and dropped it back onto the wicker cube. Was there anything here that helped him? He wasn't sure. Could Richard know something about Arthur that no one else did? Everyone felt that Arthur was a good old boy, like Walter. Or was it Jason he was describing? Or even himself? The dynamics seemed like an eerie reference to the present, whichever way you looked at it.

But that last paragraph—now, that one seemed like a direct reference to the past, to Jack Hunter and Gwen, and their love for each other. Maybe tomorrow, at the library, he'd find out more about them as well.

Chapter 15

Richard woke up with a start. He heard a rustling sound in the kitchen and saw a faint light shining from under his door. He got up, put on his bathrobe and slippers, and went out.

"Aunt Kathy, are you okay?"

"What? Oh, yes, I'm fine, Richard. As fine as you could expect."

He could see that she'd been crying. "Can I get you anything?"

"No, I just can't sleep. I thought a cup of tea might help."

Richard pulled up a chair and sat down next to his aunt. "It's going to take time, you know."

"Oh, I know, all right. Haven't I been through worse than this before, losing Tom? He was everything to me—the best husband, my best friend. What would you know about it, anyway, telling me it'll take time!"

Richard winced. Mrs. Berger must have noticed it, because she immediately apologized. "Oh, Richard, I'm sorry. You do know, losing both your parents so young. You know how unfair it is, don't you, to have to lose anything more—when you've already done your share of grieving."

"Yes," said Richard, coldly. "I know how unfair it is."

"But it's just you and me now, Richard. You're all I have left that's family. We have to be here for each other, you know. Take care of each other. I want you to know that I understand my responsibility to you, and I hope you understand your responsibility as well."

"What do you think my responsibility is, Aunt Kathy?"

"Well, I can't manage this farm by myself, you know that. I was hoping you'd consider moving back. You already understand how to manage things. And you could still write, you know. You could write here as well as in Boston—better, I'd think. It's quieter. Don't writers always come out to the country to write?"

Richard felt his stomach turn at the thought of moving back here. "We'll talk about all this later, Aunt Kathy. It may not be the best thing for you to even keep the farm now."

"What do you mean by that? You don't want to get me upset now, do you? You know how fond I've always been of you. You look so much like my Tom, you know. Jason took after *my* side of the family."

"I just mean that I understand what you're saying. That we both have to accept our responsibility toward each other. But let's just wait until Jason's in the ground before we start talking about replacing him with me."

Mrs. Berger winced this time, and started to cry.

Richard sighed. He patted his aunt's hand and spoke more softly this time. "You know as well as I do that I'm not the best one to do that, anyway—to replace him. Let's just wait a bit to see what's best for everyone, that's all I'm saying. Okay?"

Mrs. Berger nodded. Her sobbing tapered off, and she took a sip of her tea. And the two of them sat there, in silence.

Chapter 16

Smith and Marie walked through the small parking lot to the one-story green building that housed the library. Smith opened the door and Marie walked in ahead of him. He felt the coolness of the air conditioning and made sure to close the door behind him.

Moving ahead of Marie, Smith briefly noted that the walls of the library were filled with windows and that the large room was very bright. He approached the woman who was sitting behind a counter that separated the entranceway from the rest of the library.

"Hello," she said, smiling.

Smith smiled back at the petite woman with short grey hair and a twinkle in her blue eyes.

"I wonder if Beth is in?" Smith asked.

The woman's smile was replaced by a frown. "No, she won't be in today. Can I help you?" Her tone of voice had become very cool.

"We're friends of the Lynne's, and I was just wondering—"

"Oh," said the woman, her smile returning, "you guys must be the policeman from San Francisco and his wife."

Smith and Marie both laughed.

"That's us," said Marie.

"I thought for a minute you were reporters from Mountlake or something. Anyway, no, Beth's not quite ready to come back. I'm Ella."

"Hello, Ella," said Smith. "It's nice to meet you. Have you worked here a long time?"

"Ever since I retired, and before that, on and off, since I was a girl."

"You must have known Gwendolyn Gerber then—the woman who started the library."

"Oh, my goodness, of course I did. She was a saint, you know, I'm sure of it. She single-handedly got this town off its derrière to get this library started. It wasn't located here at first, of course. It started out as a storefront on Main Street. Anyway, she was the kind of person who got people moving, but not in a pushy way, if you know what I mean, but because people respected her so much, you know, even in the days when women's opinions didn't count for much—officially, at least. She was so good, you know, that she brought out the same in other people. And not in a phony way. She was the real thing."

"Was she a sad person, though? I heard she never recovered from her loss."

"No, not sad. And I wouldn't say she never recovered so much as she never accepted it. She knew she and Jack would be together again someday. It was like he was away on a business trip, and she was going about her life, not a care in the world. She loved life—she was full of life, not sad. It was also her sparkle that drew people to her, you know. Not just her goodness."

"I wish I could have known her," said Marie.

"Have you met Beth?" asked Ella.

"No, but Jeremy has."

"Well," said Ella, "she reminds me a lot of Gwennie. But I guess you wouldn't be able to tell that right now. Her light is a little dimmed by her worrying. Usually, though, she's a bright light, and she's as good as gold." She paused. "You know, it's funny I never saw this before, but Arthur reminds me quite a bit of Jack—Jack Hunter. He's got his same calm manner and kind heart, and that twinkle in his eye—always with a smile. And he's smart as a whip, just like Jack was. I think they call it 'old souls.' That's what they are, the four of them."

Smith hesitated, trying not to offend with his next question. "It seems that a lot of the boys around here recognized that quality in Beth, too," said Smith. "It's good to hear that boys are still interested in someone with character these days. There's Arthur and Jason, and even Richard, I guess—Jason's cousin?"

"Oh, Richard, yes. I guess he had his crush on Beth too, in high school. All the kids in town come through here, you know, and I get to see them all grow up. I spent a lot of time with Jason when he was small. After his father died, he came to the library a lot. His mom had her own pain to deal with and couldn't give him much support at first. Sometimes, he'd just sit, staring, not even reading. He had temper tantrums then, but I told him that wasn't the way to deal with his pain and that he had to find another way. It helps to have someone to talk to when you lose someone. That's why it was lucky for Jason's mom that Richard was here. She didn't have to face Jason's death alone."

"Lucky?" said Smith, confused. "Didn't he come down here on purpose, to be with Mrs. Berger now?"

"Well, I'm sure he would have. At least, I think so. But no, he was here already. I saw him the day before it happened, over by his old family home. I don't live far from there. He still owns it, you know, but he rents it out. He stays with his aunt when he visits. It's vacant now, though."

Smith had to hold perfectly still, even holding his breath, to keep his face from showing any emotion. He slowly let his breath out through his nose. He could see Marie in his peripheral vision and was pleased to see that she maintained a passive face as well.

"Well," said Smith, "that *was* lucky then. Anyway, I'm wondering if Beth will still be going to Jenny's wedding today. Maybe I'll see her there."

"Maybe. I don't know. Is there anything else in particular you wanted?"

"No, we just had heard how nice the library was and came in to see it. Since I've met Beth, I wanted to say hello."

"Especially the children's room," said Marie. "It's supposed to be great. I'd love to see it."

"It's downstairs," said Ella, "but Mary Louise is holding Storytime for the little ones right now—the preschoolers. She has one for the older kids on Tuesdays—well, older as in first and second grade. She'll be done in about a half hour or so. You can wait." She pointed over to a sitting area with a sofa and very comfortable looking club chairs.

Smith looked at Marie and moved his head slightly back toward the door. The movement was barely perceptible. Marie turned back to Ella.

"There really isn't time now, I know," she said. "I do want to look around though. I'll try to come back after lunch. Or, no, there's not time then either. Maybe on Monday."

"We'll see you later," said Smith. "It was nice talking to you."

"Come on in, anytime. Here are the hours."

Smith took the paper Ella handed him, smiled, and turned toward the door, which he opened, letting Marie walk through ahead of him again.

Once outside, Marie couldn't contain herself. "Jeremy, *that* was a surprise!"

Smith shook his head as they started to walk. "Let's walk over to the barracks to tell Bob. I don't want to bother Tony again, and I wouldn't want to talk about this on the bookstore phone anyway. Damn, I wish my cell phone worked here. That's the only frustrating thing about this area. Anyway, then we can grab some lunch and head back to the RV to get ready for the wedding." Smith tapped Marie's arm. "We turn here."

They turned up the same street that led to the Lynne's house.

"I *do* still want to see the children's room at the library," said Marie. "I love those little, tiny tables and chairs!

And I'd like to look up some of my favorite books." She looked at her watch and sighed. "They're closed on Sunday, but I guess I'll have time on Monday. Or even on Tuesday morning, before we go, if we don't leave too early."

After about two minutes of walking in silence, Smith tapped Marie's arm. "Here it is."

They walked through another small parking lot and entered the lone, one-story building that it serviced. Inside the entryway, another door led to a large, cluttered room where a young, stocky, sandy-haired man in a state trooper's uniform, who looked to be in his late twenties, sat behind one of the two desks behind the counter. There was also a large conference table in the room that was covered with papers.

"Hi, Jimmy," said Smith. "It's good to see you again. Is Bob in?"

"Hey, guys. No, you just missed him. He went to have a talk with Richard. I guess he wants to find out if Richard knows whether or not *Mrs. Berger* knew that Beth and Jason broke up."

"Oh, Jimmy," said Smith, urgently. "I need to talk to him before he gets there."

"No problem."

Jimmy walked over to a table stacked with radio equipment. He sat down, reached for a microphone, and pushed some buttons.

"Hey, Bob," he said into the mike. "I got Jeremy Smith here. He needs to talk to you."

"Hi, Jeremy," came Bob's voice over the speaker. "What's up? I'm on my way to talk to Richard."

"I know. But I've got something for you. Richard was already here the day before Jason died."

"What! I don't believe it. He didn't say a word—neither of them did. How do you know?"

"Ella, at the library, saw him at his old house—his parent's house, I guess."

"Yeah, she lives near there. Well, that puts a different spin on things. You know, it doesn't change the evidence, but it definitely could lead somewhere. I'm glad I found this out *before* I spoke to him. Thanks again, Jeremy. I appreciate your keeping your ear to the ground for me."

"No problem. Let me know how it goes, if you get the chance, will you?"

"You bet I will. If there's nothing urgent, I'll just tell you later at the wedding."

"Sounds good. See you then."

"Right. And Jimmy," Penny added sharply, "don't mention this to anyone. I don't want anyone else to know about it yet."

"Will do."

Smith was surprised at Penny's tone of voice, but Jimmy didn't seem to be fazed by it. He looked up at Smith with a grin. "Well, that's something!"

"Yeah," said Smith.

"Will you be at the wedding today, Jimmy?" asked Marie.

"No, I'll be right here, and on patrol."

"Well," said Smith, "thanks for your help. Maybe we'll see you again before we leave."

"When are you leaving?"

"Probably Tuesday."

"Maybe not. I'm working tomorrow, but I'm off Monday and Tuesday."

"Well," said Marie, "just in case, then, it was nice meeting you."

"You, too," said Jimmy. "You guys have a safe trip back home."

"Thanks," they said.

Smith and Marie left the building and headed back toward Main Street.

"With all this going on," said Marie, "maybe we can put off leaving until Wednesday."

"I don't know that it would make a difference, but thanks for offering. Let's just wait and see how it goes. That's the gypsy life we're leading!"

"When we get back to the RV park, I'll ask if they have room for us to stay the extra day, just in case."

"Good idea, but let's still grab a quick lunch now. I know we need to get ready for the wedding soon, but I'm starved."

Chapter 17

Bob Penny was a little different, as police officers went. Unlike the cynicism that some developed when they dealt with the darker side of human nature, Penny preferred to maintain the same optimistic view of the world that he had held since childhood.

The down side of this accomplishment was that, unlike Smith, who maintained his equanimity through an intellectualized understanding of and compassion for humanity, including its foibles, Penny became grumpy when forced to deal with more than the usual number of serious infractions that cropped up in a rural area. Partly, he had moved here to avoid the violence that went along with the larger population in a congested city environment.

This was not to say that he wasn't capable of addressing more serious crimes. He was very capable. He was just grumpy.

Penny liked the people in this town. He liked Beth and Arthur. He had liked Jason. He didn't know Richard as well, but he liked him. The thought that either Arthur killed Jason or else Richard, or someone else, killed him and framed Arthur made him grumpy.

Turning onto Mrs. Berger's property, Penny noted that both vehicles were present—Richard's Avalon and Mrs. Burger's GMC pickup. Before he went in, he closed his eyes and took a deep breath. He wasn't sure exactly how he was going to approach this interview, and he didn't like that feeling. His first instinct had been to focus on other things first, and then to casually ask Richard where he was on Wednesday and Thursday. Then, if Richard lied, he'd spring the news on him that he was busted. But then, thinking about it, he worried that, if Richard became suspicious from the initial questions, he might guess what was coming and have time to come up with an explanation.

No, he had better start with the big guns. He got out of the car and stretched, like a fighter going into the ring. Ignoring the dog that came up to him to say hello—another sign of his current, grumpy status—he knocked on the door. Richard answered the knock.

"Hi, Bob, come on in."

Penny followed Richard into the living room. They both sat down, Richard on the couch, and Penny facing him on the club chair that was the only other piece of furniture in the room. There wasn't even a coffee table. Looking around for a moment, Penny had the thought that the dinginess of the room—the sparseness and age of the furnishings—seemed to match the mood of the place.

"So," said Richard, "I know you've arrested Arthur. I still can't believe it. I thought my aunt was just talking nonsense—because of her grief and all."

"Actually," said Penny, keeping a calm, unconcerned look on his face, "that's why I arranged for this talk. But something else has come up." He paused.

"Yes," said Richard, mirroring Penny's friendly look and tone of voice.

"You were here the day before Jason died. Why did you lie?"

Richard's face froze, and the color drained out of it. Then he hesitated, as if he were going to argue but thought better of it. Before he spoke, he glanced over toward the closed door of his aunt's bedroom. "I don't know that I actually lied so much as let you assume I had come to town in response to my aunt's call." He spoke very quietly. "Technically, she did call me on my cell, and I was almost halfway home when she called. She doesn't even know that I'd been here already."

Penny continued to stare silently at Richard.

Richard took a deep breath, and glanced over at the door again. "Look, I was here to check on my rental property. My aunt manages it for me, and I … well, I'd been losing tenants too often lately. I was beginning to worry that she may not have been doing the upkeep and repairs that you need to do to *keep* a good tenant—though she did charge me for repairs that were supposedly done. I guess I wanted to see for myself what condition the building was in. I didn't want my aunt to know I was here because I didn't want her to think I didn't trust her. And also, I wasn't going to stop and see them—her and Jason—this trip at all, so I *couldn't* let her know I was here."

Penny digested what Richard had said.

"You say you were halfway home?"

"Yes, I stayed at the house overnight, and I left the next day, at around lunchtime."

"Can you prove that?"

Richard paused before answering, tightening his cheeks and raising his eyes up and to the right, as if trying to remember. "No, I don't think so. I didn't think I'd have to. I filled up with gas locally, but that doesn't prove anything. I paid cash at the bridges and tollbooths. I never keep receipts on that stuff. Look, why are you even asking me this? I told you why I was here. You already arrested Arthur. If you don't have the evidence he did it, why did you arrest him? If you do, why are you worrying about me?"

Penny knew that Richard had raised a good point. He couldn't tell him that he just didn't want it to be Arthur, or that he couldn't bring himself to believe he had missed the hammer when he searched the area on the day Jason died. He didn't really want to think it was Richard either. And even though it seemed suspicious that Richard was here on that day and had hidden it, his explanation, unfortunately for Arthur, did make sense. Penny would check up on the tenant situation in the house to make sure that this part of Richard's story was true, but barring a problem with that information, there really wasn't much more to say about it.

"I'm not worrying, Richard. I just have to check up on anything that seems out of the ordinary surrounding a murder. If you could prove when you had left, it would just dot an "i" for me, but you're right, it doesn't change anything. There *is* one more thing I wanted to talk to you about, though. Did you know that Jason and Beth had broken up, and that she had started seeing Arthur again?"

"No, I didn't! Well, that doesn't make sense. Are you sure, because why did Arthur kill him then? I mean, I just assumed, if he did it, which is still hard for me to believe, that the motive would be some kind of jealousy or something—that something must have snapped in him. He couldn't have been in his right mind."

Penny began to feel that Richard, also, was extremely sincere in his confusion, a confusion that matched Arthur's. And he really did seem to want to support Arthur, even though it was his own cousin who was dead. He acted like he wanted to be sure of the truth, and not to get revenge on someone—anyone—just to feel better.

"So your aunt never mentioned knowing about it either, then."

"No, and I don't think she would have been so positive that Arthur killed Jason if she did know. Are you sure it's even true? Who told you?" A light went on in Richard's eyes. "Is that what they're saying—Beth and Arthur? Well, if no one else knows but them, that sounds a little suspicious to me, like she's protecting him. God, maybe he *did* do it."

Penny suddenly realized he needed to find out for sure if anyone else did know. He had let that slip by him, counting on Mrs. Berger to corroborate Beth's story about telling *her,* and also knowing that, even if it were corroborated, it didn't prove that Arthur didn't kill Jason. Arthur could still have been jealous. Or he could have been responding to an attack by Jason or protecting Beth.

"I didn't say no one else knew. I wanted to know if *you* knew. Well, I guess that's it, except I need to ask your aunt also, while I'm here. I hate to bother her—"

"I wish you wouldn't."

"I wish I didn't have to, but it'll just be one question. Could you call her out here for me?"

Richard hesitated as if he were going to protest again, but in the end, he got up. Walking through the kitchen, he knocked on the bedroom door.

"Aunt Kathy?"

"Yes, Richard, what is it?" Mrs. Berger's voice sounded more irritated that injured.

"Bob Penny's here. He just has one question for you. Could you come out?"

"Oh, what now? Oh, fine! I'll be right there."

Mrs. Berger may not have sounded like she was wounded, but looking at her face when she came out of her room, tying up a bathrobe around her, there was no question that she was in a lot of emotional pain. Maybe, thought Penny, it was her pain that was making her irritable.

"Hello, Mrs. Berger. Would you like to sit down?"

"No, I wouldn't. Richard said it was just one question, so ask it and let me get back to my room."

Penny hesitated for just a moment, gathering his thoughts.

"It's just that, I wondered if you remembered what time it was that Beth came by here the day Jason died?" Penny ignored the look of confusion on Richard's face but was happy that he didn't open his mouth. Penny was getting irritable again himself. He mentally shook himself and concentrated on Mrs. Berger's response. She definitely was not surprised by the question. She seemed to think for a moment, and then she answered matter-of-factly.

"I guess it was around eleven or so—before lunch, at least. Why?"

"I just need to check on everyone's movements, more or less. But also, when she told you she had broken up with Jason, were you worried at all that Jason might have been upset or angry?"

"I don't know what you're talking about."

Despite her words, Mrs. Berger didn't look or sound at all confused. She was still very matter-of-fact.

"You mean you had no reason to worry about Jason? He was okay with it?"

"I mean I don't know what you're talking about. She never said any such thing. She just came by to say hello. She did that every now and then. And that's nonsense, anyway. Jason would have told me if they broke up. He was a sensitive boy—" She stopped, and for the first time, for only a fleeting moment, she looked nervous. "He was very sensitive to my feelings, I mean. He was a good son. He knew how fond I was of Beth and would have told me."

"But they did break up—"

"If that's true, I didn't know anything about it. And if *I* didn't know, *Jason* didn't know. Now, that was two questions, if I'm not mistaken, and I'm going back to bed. The next time I want to see you, Bob Penny, is when you tell me when the trial is set for."

With that, Kathy Berger turned on her heel and marched back into her room, closing the door forcefully behind her.

Penny looked over at Richard, who immediately avoided his gaze. *He's not sure about his aunt either*, Penny thought. *But her affect hasn't been quite right about anything since her son died.*

Richard motioned toward the door and started to walk. "Well, I hope you got everything you need. Tell Arthur I don't hate him, would you, Bob. I just can't bring myself to go see him. Especially now. I really don't know what to think. I'm not as skeptical as I was at first about your having arrested him."

They reached the door, and Richard opened it. Penny walked out and then turned back. "I'll keep you both informed of the progress of the case," he said.

"Thanks," said Richard, still avoiding eye contact as he closed the door.

Penny looked at his watch and walked back to the patrol car, sure of only two things. One was that, unlike Richard, he couldn't say he was less skeptical of the case against Arthur—well, maybe a little, though he certainly wasn't *more* skeptical of it. And the other thing was that he had to get home to get ready for a wedding.

Chapter 18

Smith and Marie pulled onto the Lynne's property, amazed at the transformation. Straight ahead, just past the rows of cars that were parked in a field to the right, was a large, white tent covering at least two dozen tables, all set with white tablecloths.

"I knew the property was large," said Smith, "but this really shows how large it is. And that's just the lawn, not the wooded area."

"I've never seen such a large tent at a private home," said Marie. "And tablecloths! I hope they don't blow away in the wind."

"It's not that windy," said Smith, "and I'm glad to see the tent. It's past the worst heat of the day, but the sun is still pretty strong."

Holding hands, the two walked toward a group of people who were gathered at one end of the tent. There, they found a small cart with a seating chart, place cards, and a map of the tables. It turned out that there were actually thirty-three of them, and currently they were blocked off with braided cord. Also, an open bar had been set up for wine and cocktails, and there were servers walking around with trays of appetizers. All these things explained the gathering of people here.

As he reached for an appetizer, Smith heard Marie gasp. "What is it?" he asked.

"Look!" Marie had stepped to the side and was pointing past the group of milling people.

Following her gaze, Smith saw what had impressed her. Beyond the tent, rows of chairs, all decorated with white and pink lace, were set up in a semicircle in front of a grove of trees, within which was set up a smaller canopy and an altar. Beyond the grove, the ground sloped down, revealing, far in the distance, rows of rolling, green hills and mountaintops and a beautiful, wide-open, deep blue sky, dotted with soft, floating mounds of white—the beauty of the Catskill Mountains.

At some signal unseen to Smith, people started to move toward the altar. He took a quick look at the seating chart and noted that he and Marie would be with Bob Penny and his wife at table number twenty-seven, and that there were two other names at their table that he recognized as being state troopers who were friends of the Lynne's—or else, one may have been with the sheriff's department.

"It looks like they're keeping all their policemen at the same table," said Smith, scooping up his and Marie's place cards. "They probably don't want to make anyone else uncomfortable!"

Marie laughed. "That's one way to group people, I guess. I wonder if there'll be a financial adviser for me to talk to. Or a nurse, maybe. But I'm glad we're sitting with Bob. I like him, and I'm looking forward to meeting Maggie."

They found a seat and looked around expectantly. The easy-listening music that was playing when they arrived had stopped. Smith saw Tony sitting a few rows ahead of them, but he didn't recognize anyone else yet. As more and more people filled the seats, he looked around for Bob Penny, but he didn't see him. He didn't see Beth White or Ella from the library either.

Smith had time to marvel at how easily the guests had been directed to the altar and away from the tables, and at how well the altar had been placed, like a stage. Something began to tickle the back of Smith's brain, or itch was more like it—an itch he couldn't scratch. Then, the minister moved into the grove of trees, followed by the groom and the best man. Smith recognized the groom from a photograph at the Lynne's house.

Softly at first, the song "You Light Up My Life" began to play, and the pageant began. Smith smiled to himself at the choice of song, which so matched the environment around him. This thought made his brain itch stronger.

The pageant progressed, from the mothers of the bride and groom, escorted by the groom's father; to the bridesmaids and the ushers; to the flower girl, giggling as she spread flowers along the aisle; to the maid of honor; and finally, to Jenny—lovely, petite, brown-haired Jenny, all in white—on the arm of her father, who looked more proud than Smith had ever seen him. It was beautiful, well choreographed, emotional—and Smith was not any the less moved because it was what he expected to see.

Expected—

Smith's brain itch could be ignored no longer. He was only barely aware of the remainder of the ceremony—his brain going into "percolator" mode, as his ex-colleague Fred Wong had dubbed it, letting all of the facts steep and brew, becoming stronger and clearer.

Smith did see Jenny get kissed, and he took this as a sign that it was time to come back to the present moment. He glanced over at Marie, who had tears in her eyes, and smiled. When the guests all rose, Smith looked behind him and saw Bob Penny standing in the back, his arm entwined with that of a tall, slim woman with short, black hair. He caught his eye, and they nodded at each other. The guests began to file out behind the newly married couple and their entourage. Smith didn't see Penny again until they got to the table, where he and Maggie were already seated. Penny stood up.

"Jeremy, hi, I guess we get to spend a *lot* more time together. I hope you're not sick of me yet, considering how much I interrupted your vacation."

"No, of course not."

"No," added Marie. "We like you. Is this Maggie?"

"Oh, excuse me, yes," said Penny. "Maggie, this is Jeremy and Marie Smith."

"I figured that out," said Maggie, with a smile. She stood up and shook hands with Smith and Marie. "It's nice to meet you both. Bob has such nice things to say about you. And Jeremy, I'm told that you know my absolute most favorite director in the world. I have to talk to you about him."

"I'm not sure I have much to tell you, other than what a nice guy he is."

"Oh, Marie," said Penny, "besides Maggie's interest in acting, she's also a loan officer in a bank, so you two have a little in common there. You're a financial planner, aren't you?"

"Yes, I am." Marie got the words out before her laughter bubbled up out of her, as she leaned toward Smith, saying, "Close enough."

Smith laughed back, and then noticed the confusion on the Penny's faces. "Marie, why don't you explain why we're laughing to Maggie, while I take Bob away for a couple of minutes. Would you mind, Bob?"

"No, of course not."

Marie sat down in the chair on the other side of Maggie from where Bob had been sitting, saying, "Hurry back, though."

"Yes, don't be *too* long, please, guys," said Maggie. "It's Saturday, and this *is* Jenny's wedding, you know."

"We know," said Smith. "We'll be right back."

Penny followed Smith out from under the tent, and they walked another twenty feet or so. "What's up?" Penny asked.

"I've been thinking, and I have some ideas. I wonder if you'd mind telling me what happened when you talked to Richard."

"Sure, I wanted to tell you about it. He says he was up here to check on his rental property. Kathy Berger manages it for him, and he hasn't been able to hold a tenant lately. He was nervous about the condition of the place—maybe tenants were leaving because things weren't being kept up—and he came here to check it out. He didn't want Mrs. Berger to know because he didn't want her to think he didn't trust her, which he doesn't, and he didn't want to stop in and see her this trip, either. He says he had already left to drive back to Boston before Jason died, and was halfway home when Mrs. Berger called him."

"I see. That *is* plausible, I guess." Smith didn't sound totally convinced. "Can he prove the timing?"

"Nope. No gas receipts. No toll receipts. But he seemed truthful, and he even acted like he didn't think Arthur would kill Jason—he almost defended him."

"Well, that could indicate guilt as well as innocence. But how about Mrs. Berger?"

"She agrees that Beth saw her the day Jason died, but denies that Beth told her they had broken up. She insists Jason would have told her if it were true. But she wasn't surprised enough by the idea, somehow, I didn't think. Her answer sounded a little rehearsed. The only time she showed any emotion, other than annoyance, was when she started to say that Jason was a "sensitive boy"—she looked nervous for a minute and changed it to "sensitive to his mother's feelings.""

Another idea bubbled up into Smith's awareness. "Well, that's all very interesting. I have a few ideas, and this seems to narrow them down a little. Maybe not. Look, I really don't want you to feel that I'm sticking my nose in or anything—"

"I pretty much invited your nose in. Don't worry about it."

Smith smiled briefly. "Well, in that case, I'm thinking that even if it was Mrs. Berger, technically, who was managing Richard's rental, it might have been Jason who dealt with the money or interacted with the tenants. You said Mrs. Berger told you Jason managed the business aspects of the farm?"

Penny nodded. "I think I see where you're going with this. If there was a problem with money, there could have been an altercation between Jason and Richard."

"Exactly. But also, if there was a problem with a tenant, the problem could have been between the tenant and Jason."

"Of course! So I should be talking to past tenants as well! I'll look into both possibilities tomorrow morning. I'll ask Richard and Mrs. Berger about who did what on the rental and about what the financial situation is, although she said she didn't want to see me again unless I was telling her when the trial was set for!"

Smith couldn't help but laugh. He had faced a similar reception many times.

"And also," continued Penny, "I'll get a list of past tenants and look them up. Thanks, Jeremy, I really appreciate how you think."

"You're welcome, but there's also one favor I'd like to ask you for."

"Good! What?"

"Do you think I could have a chance to talk to Arthur tomorrow, at your convenience?"

Penny thought for a moment. "I don't see why not. But he's being held in the correctional facility in Mountlake. It's just a few blocks from where I'm based out of—where we first brought him."

"That's okay with me, and I appreciate it."

"Would you mind telling me what it's about?"

"I'd rather wait until tomorrow, if you don't mind. I'm not really sure how to put it in words yet, and I need to add what you've just told me into the mix."

"Okay, then. It'll probably be tomorrow afternoon sometime. I'll call you in the morning after I've set it up. Maybe I can even drive you, although it looks like I'll be pretty busy tomorrow."

"That would be great. I can explain what I'm thinking in the car on the way there."

"Perfect," said Penny. "Now, I think we'd better get back to our wives."

"That's for sure! And besides, I'm starved."

When they got back to the table, they found that Jenny and David, the groom, were using their seats. They were making the rounds, greeting people.

"Jenny!" said Smith. "Congratulations. You look beautiful."

"Uncle Jeremy." Jenny got up and threw herself into Smith's arms. "I'm so glad you're here. And I love Marie! Maggie and I have decided that you could not have done better for yourself."

Marie laughed. "Thank you."

"I already *know* that," said Smith. "But I'm not the only lucky newlywed we've got here. David, hello from one lucky man to another. I'm Jeremy Smith." He held out his hand.

"Oh, I forgot," said Jenny, "you haven't met. But I've told him all about you."

"Doesn't anybody want to tell Bob how lucky *he* is?" said Maggie.

"I'll be happy to do that," said Marie.

"Well, if you hadn't, I would have myself," said Bob. "You don't have to be a newlywed to feel lucky in love, you know!"

"That's good to hear," said Smith, before turning back to Jenny. "I know you guys have a lot of people to visit with at the wedding, and then you're off on your honeymoon tonight. If I don't get to talk to you again this trip, I want you to know how happy I was that Marie and I could be here and see this."

"I'm happy too, but actually, David wanted to talk to you about something privately. Do you have a minute?"

Smith looked hungrily down at his salad and hid his disappointment. "Of course," he said. "Right this way." Smith turned and led David back outside the tent. "So, David, I hope it's not the birds and the bees you're wanting to know about. It's a little late in the game for that lesson."

David laughed. "No, it's just that ... Well, like you said, Jenny and I are leaving, so this may be my last chance to say something to Bob that I'm not sure I should say, and Jenny suggested I ask you first."

"Okay. Shoot."

"It's about Jason. He's a little older than Jenny and me, but my older brother was a friend of his, so we still talk sometimes—talked, I guess. Anyway, he was a good guy, really he was. He cared about doing the right thing, you know, *that* kind of guy. But he was acting funny ... oh, for the last few weeks or so, I'd guess. He seemed to be almost nasty. I never saw that in him before. He was being very rude to people, and he pissed some people off. I'm not saying it means anything, and I'm not sure I should say anything about it. I mean, there's no one specifically I can name as being mad at him or anything. It's just that, the way he was acting, there *could* have been, you know."

Smith looked closely at David. "You're sure there's no one specific? It's important, David."

"No, I'm sure. Nothing happened worth killing him over. But he may have lost a friend or two."

"I see. Well, I would suggest that you *do* tell this to Bob. Even just understanding Jason's frame of mind can be helpful. I'm glad you decided to talk about it. And like you said, his behavior wasn't worth killing him over. If he *was* killed, he didn't deserve to be, and anything that can help bring justice to the situation needs to be looked at."

"I thought so too, I guess. But since Arthur was already arrested ... It just doesn't seem relevant now—the other people, I mean. But I don't want to make it seem like

Arthur had a reason or anything either. I mean, Arthur's not the kind of person to let someone get under his skin."

"Don't worry. It won't make it harder on him. And it could help him. As long as it's the truth, you're in safe territory."

"Okay, then. Thanks. I'll do it."

The two men returned to Smith's table.

"Bob," said David, "would you mind if I talked to you for a minute?"

Smith saw Marie and Maggie look at each other with an expression that he defined as "mutual understanding and commiseration." He held back his smile, though, and sat down nonchalantly as Bob stood up and followed David back out to the "office." Ignoring Marie's questioning glance, he picked up a fork and dug in.

Chapter 19

Penny called just as Smith was finishing breakfast the next morning. Marie was out walking the dogs.

"Hi, Bob," said Smith, swallowing his last bite of toast.

"I set it up for you to see Arthur at two. Will that work for you?"

"That's fine. I appreciate it."

"The only thing is, besides looking into the tenant angle, I'll be talking to a few of the local boys who had run-ins with Jason over the past couple of weeks, so I'm not sure I'll have time to take you."

"Oh, then David *did* end up giving you a few names?"

"Yes, but it doesn't sound like anything serious. I think the information is more interesting because it shows another side to Jason—a side Beth hinted at. There could be some unknown person who he did piss off badly and who hasn't turned up yet, like maybe one of the tenants. And it also adds weight to Beth's claim that *she's* the one who broke it off with Jason, because he seems to have been upset about *something* lately. I did check with Beth and Arthur's parents, who all say they knew it when Beth and Jason broke up, but I really need to ask around and see if anyone else can verify that. I think I'll try and talk to Mary Louise at the library. She and Beth are close."

"Bob …" Smith hesitated.

"Yeah."

"Would I be pushing it if I went and had a talk with Beth this morning also?"

Bob laughed. "I think one citizen of this country is allowed to talk to whatever other citizen they want to, barring the existence of a restraining order."

Smith smiled. "Yeah, but since she first met me in your company, and you said I was helping you, there could be an applied association this time also, and I wanted to be sure you were okay with it."

"No problem. So, if I can make it, should I pick you up at your RV—say, one o'clock?"

"Perfect. I'll be here."

"I'll call if I can't come. Can you find it yourself?"

"Yes. I've still got the cocktail napkin with your directions from yesterday. Don't rush, and I'll see you later."

Penny laughed. "Right. Bye."

Smith put the phone in his shirt pocket, grabbed a writing pad and a pen, and went outside. Their RV site had a picnic bench and a tree, and he decided to take advantage of both. He sat in a shady spot and started to think.

Basically, his big insight yesterday was a simple one. This entire murder seemed as staged as the wedding had been, only the script wasn't out of a wedding manual—it was Richard Tomlinson's book. The question is, was the murder patterned after the book, or was it made to match the book after the fact?

Given the people involved so far, what were the possible scenarios? Always remembering that there could be someone else unknown still involved, he decided to write it all out, as if he still had the blackboard back at Homicide.

Okay, then. First, let's look at the possibility that Arthur was framed.

Smith wrote this possibility down on a clean page, under which he wrote:

1. Some unknown person—someone who, not realizing that Jason and Beth had broken up, thought Arthur was the perfect person to frame. They could have stolen Arthur's hammer in advance. It would have needed to be someone who had read the book—maybe an old tenant of Richard's.

2. Richard—He had been complaining that the townspeople were angry about the book without even reading it, so his own words served to add him to this list. He was one of the few people locally who *did* know what was in his book, and he didn't think many others did. Maybe he was mad at Jason about some financial issue, like maybe Jason embezzled some of his money from the rental or something.

Or, maybe Richard did have feelings for Beth. Maybe he heard she broke up with Arthur, came down here with his hopes up, and then found out she was seeing Jason, of all people. He said he didn't know she and Jason broke up, although it did seem like he knew they had been seeing each other. Still, maybe he came down here because he decided he wasn't going to give up his chance, even to his cousin. Maybe things got out of hand, or maybe he planned the murder all along, and planned to frame Arthur all along, and stole his hammer to kill Jason.

Or, if the murder wasn't planned, he might have decided to frame Arthur after the fact. After all, that would explain why Bob didn't find the hammer on the day of Jason's death. Maybe Richard put it there after the murder.

But how would he have gotten Jason's blood and hair on it? I guess he could have had access to some of his hair, off a hairbrush or something. But he'd need to get into Jason's house without Mrs. Berger seeing him. Unless, maybe Jason had a brush or comb on him at the time. I'm not sure about how Richard would manage the blood, though. The blood is a definite sticking point to the framing theory—it was hard to it explain it unless the hammer really was the murder weapon, or at least present at the murder.

3. Arthur—Yes, even Arthur had to be on this list. He could have come up with the idea that framing himself by imitating the book with the hammer would make him seem innocent. We know from Richard that Arthur read the book.

4. Beth—It would be hard to believe, but maybe Jason was really the love of her life. Maybe she was only pretending to still care about Arthur. Maybe she knew Arthur had killed Jason and wanted to make sure he was caught and punished—that would also be "lying for love." Or maybe she hated both of them. Maybe she stole Arthur's hammer and killed Jason with it. Her alibi isn't that strong. Maybe she got that store receipt some other way.

Smith set the pen down and laughed. It seemed that everyone involved made it to this list, except Jason's mom and Bob. If he wanted to, he could even add Tony to it, because Tony had read the book.

And come to think of it, why didn't Bob find that hammer the first day? No, that's crazy. But wait ...

Smith picked up the pen again.

5. Mrs. Berger—Maybe she knew that Richard killed her son, but in a way that she didn't blame him—an accident or defending himself—and she didn't want to lose her nephew too. Maybe she thought the best way to keep Richard safe was to frame someone else—to point the finger at Arthur, like she did from the beginning. And maybe the reason she claimed she didn't believe Jason and Beth had broken up—that she denied Beth told her—was to make that accusation stronger—to keep alive a motive for Arthur.

There! Now I've got everyone. Okay, what's next?

On a fresh page, Smith wrote: Arthur is guilty.

So, what evidence is there to support this?

1. Hammer—belongs to Arthur, has Arthur's fingerprints, has victim's hair and blood.

Smith scowled. *Case closed! What am I even doing here?* Sighing, he continued.

2. Motive—Maybe Arthur didn't know Beth and Jason broke up, or maybe they hadn't really, and Beth was covering for him now—taking away his motive. Or maybe

Jason attacked Arthur because Beth did break up with him. Though, if it was self-defense, Smith didn't see Arthur hiding it to this extent, though some people got frightened and did. But if Jason said or did something to enrage Arthur, and Arthur killed him for it, that's not self-defense. Maybe Jason even threatened Beth.

I guess I just don't see Arthur killing Jason with a hammer, up by the falls, coincidentally just like in the book. I feel like someone is staging a murder, just like the wedding was staged, based on people's expectations—in this case, based on expectations about a "love triangle." So, I'm looking for someone else who could have staged it. I don't really see Arthur doing it at all, to be honest, except in self-defense, and I don't see him hiding it if it were self-defense. Unless he's got me fooled and he's a sociopath or something, which would be just like the book again.

But also, looking at it another way, if he did kill Jason, I don't see him leaving the hammer there—unless he was framing himself, or not realizing it fell out of his pocket, or something. I only see it being left behind by accident if it was an unplanned murder, and someone was running out of there in a panic. Who would do that and also have Arthur's hammer, except Arthur?

Smith froze. An idea was just outside the reach of his consciousness. He didn't force it. He let it slide right in.

It wouldn't be unbelievable for a hammer of Arthur's to have been at Beth's house with his fingerprints still on it. They had dated for years. Then, while Jason was dating Beth, certainly there could have been some circumstance where Jason ended up with it. Could Jason have had the hammer with him, and someone unknown used it as a weapon of opportunity to kill him?

If it was unplanned, the killer could have been in a panic. Whether done in anger or not, if someone thought the hammer was Jason's, they might not have thought they needed or wanted to keep it with them long enough to get rid of it. Maybe they had gloves on and weren't worried about prints—work gloves or fishing gloves or something.

But why wouldn't Arthur or Beth have mentioned this possibility? Maybe even *they* didn't think of it. The hammer could have been at Beth's house for years.

Well, he hoped that the next person he would be talking to about all this was Beth. He would try to connect with her as soon as Marie got back with the dogs.

Chapter 20

Marie had decided she wanted to take the dogs into town, so Smith dropped them off first and then drove on to Beth's house. He collected his thoughts. What was it he wanted to know about Beth White? What did he hope to gain from this interview?

First of all, whom did she love? Was her love for Arthur real?

If it was, did she know this before Jason died? Did she really break up with Jason? Could she be making that up to help Arthur now? Would all four parents go along with that story? And she said the other day that her breaking up with Jason didn't have anything to do with Arthur. If she did break up with Jason, why did she, and what motive might Arthur still have had to kill him—or might *she* have had?

If she didn't love Arthur, did she love Jason? Could she be trying to harm Arthur without his knowing it? Or did she hate both of them enough to kill one and frame the other?

And someone was lying. Either Beth was lying and she didn't tell Mrs. Berger that she and Jason broke up and that she was worried about him, or else Mrs. Berger was lying. That really was the crux of it. If you find a lie, it can be like an arrow, pointing to the truth. Unfortunately, though, sometimes it just pointed to another lie.

Finally, Smith hoped to come to some conclusion about whether Arthur's hammer might have gotten into Jason's hands somehow.

Feeling prepared, he took a deep breath and got out of the car. The front door was closed this time. He rang the doorbell and a man answered. He was about Smith's age and height, but with a much slighter frame. He looked like he could be Marie's brother, so Smith supposed he must be Beth's father.

"Mr. White?"

"Yes, you must be Jeremy Smith. Come in. Beth's expecting you." He stepped aside to let Smith in, closing the door behind him. "How's Arthur, do you know?"

"I think he's holding up okay. I'll be seeing him this afternoon."

"Oh, good. Tell him I'm praying for him, will you?"

"Of course." Smith had an idea. "It sounds like you're fond of him."

"Oh, yes. He's like a son to me." Mr. White swiped at his eyes in confusion, as if not accustomed to the presence of the tears that suddenly filled them.

"I wonder," said Smith, "I know Arthur's pretty handy. Did he ever bring his tools over here to work on something for you? In all those years, he must have, I guess."

Mr. White laughed. "Come with me," he said, holding up his index finger and motioning with it for Smith to follow.

They walked into the kitchen, and Mr. White opened a door. Smith found himself looking into an attached garage, the inside of which housed a large workbench and the largest, reddest toolbox he'd ever seen. It must have weighed a thousand pounds.

"I'm pretty handy myself," said Mr. White. "I even built this garage onto the house. I don't think Arthur could've brought me any tool I didn't already have. Of course, he did help me out once in a while. I taught him quite a bit of what he knows, I would imagine."

Smith smiled. "I can see that. I wish I had your skills in that area."

Mr. White nodded, accepting the comment as his due. "So, anyway, you might as well have a seat here. I'll call Beth for you."

"I'm right here." Beth walked into the kitchen. "I wondered where you two had gone. I heard the doorbell."

"Well, we're *here* is where we are," said Mr. White. "I'll leave you both to talk. I'm going over to see Arthur's dad. Your mom'll be home from church soon."

"Okay, Dad." Beth kissed her father on the cheek, and he went into the garage. She turned to Smith and smiled. "My dad's proud of his toolbox, you know."

Smith smiled back and gave it another try. "I could see that, and he should be. I wouldn't guess you'd ever need to use someone else's tools at this house, not even one of Arthur's tools."

"Not likely."

Smith heard a car start in the garage.

"So," continued Beth, "what is it you wanted to talk about? Are you working with Bob?"

"Not officially. Just lending my talents."

Beth looked deeply into Smith's eyes and smiled. "I would guess your talents are as considerable as my fathers, in your own field, and that you're just as proud of them."

Smith smiled and nodded. He had been looking just as deeply into Beth's eyes, as well as listening very carefully to her voice. He saw and heard what he had always seen—a person of character. A sad person, but definitely her father's daughter. Marie would call her an old soul. In fact, hadn't someone already done so? Anyway, whatever mess she had gotten into here, Smith couldn't believe it was of her making. He felt he could put her at the end of his list—he didn't see her as a murderer or as someone who would frame Arthur. But he couldn't rule her out as someone who would lie to protect Arthur. Still, he had to be sure.

Beth pointed to the small, round, wooden kitchen table. "Is here okay?"

"That's fine, thanks." They sat facing each other. Smith took a moment before beginning. Looking around, he was surprised to notice that the kitchen was a modern one, unlike the rest of the house, which maintained its period charm. There even were granite countertops.

"This kitchen must reflect your father's work," said Smith. "Like the garage. I thought a two-car, attached garage was unusual in a Craftsman-style house!"

Beth smiled. "I know, it doesn't match the house. But my mother prefers an updated kitchen."

"No, it's great! I like to cook, and it would be a treat to do that in this kitchen." Smith focused back on the task at hand. "I know this is a hard time for you. As you said—to lose Arthur and get him back, and then to face losing him again."

Beth winced slightly and then quickly regained her composure. She smiled sadly, with a smile that didn't reach her eyes, and nodded.

"I don't want to cause you more pain by asking you to talk about it, but I feel that something's not quite right with this case, and so that's just what I'm going to ask you to do. Can you talk to me about Arthur—about the breakup, yes, but also about your relationship, before and after you broke up? About what there is between you."

Beth looked confused at this request, so Smith continued. "It may seem like an odd question, but there's something I need to know, and I don't exactly know what it is. If you can just talk to me, there's a chance that something you say will help Arthur. I know you want to do that."

"Of course." She took a deep breath. "Okay, I'll try." She paused, her eyes closed. When she opened them and began to speak, all of her warmth shone through. "It's like we were always together—like we've always been together. Even when we were children, before we had any romantic thoughts, it was like we completed each other. Even then, we would finish each other's sentences. But, you know, when we were older, it wasn't like anything had changed. Even our romantic feelings …"

She hesitated and looked into Smith's eyes.

He nodded. "If you don't mind."

"I guess I could try to explain it." She sighed and then continued. "Our romantic feelings were like a bud opening up into a flower. The flower was always there, inside the bud—always a part of the plant—but it opened at the right time, like it was meant to. It was never as if we were brother and sister, or anything like that. We were always a … well, a pair, I guess."

Smith was moved by Beth's description. "So tell me," he asked, "why did it come apart?"

"I don't really know—at least I didn't at the time, which was the strangest part of it. He made it seem like he wanted to see if there was something else he might prefer to do. He acted as if he were tired of feeling like he had no choice about how his life was going." She stopped.

Smith could see that Beth's memory of this time was painful for her, but he needed to understand. "Can you go on?" he asked, gently.

"Yes." Beth sat up straighter. "I can tell you that it was like every cell in my body had been ripped in half. At first, I didn't know if my lungs would have the capacity to breathe, or my heart to beat. But then, I had to accept that Arthur needed to go through his life on his own path, and I decided to go on with my own. I can't fault myself for not understanding what it really was, because I still don't understand it completely, unless he had a premonition about all of this that's gone on. But he says it was more like a memory than a premonition, and that he couldn't explain it any better than that."

"What do you mean? What was it, really?"

"When he came to see me after I had broken up with Jason—that wasn't why I broke it off with Jason at all, you know—but when he came, after, it turned out that, before Arthur broke up with me, he had become overwhelmed with a fear of being separated from me. He couldn't explain it, but he was terrified, and it was so intense that the only way he could find to block it out was to block me out. Then, what happened, of course, was that, after we were apart, he realized that he had *caused* to happen exactly what he'd been afraid of."

"A self-fulfilling prophesy," said Smith.

"Exactly. When I started seeing Jason, Arthur said he suddenly realized that his life's purpose included me, and that he had to accept the fact that this was true no matter how long or short of a time we had together. But he also thought it was too late. He said he thought he might have to live the rest of his life without me, just marking time until we could be together again."

This time Smith was confused. "When would that be?"

"I would guess in Heaven, or in the next life, or something like that. He just knew that someday we would be together again, and he wouldn't mess it up the next time. But he said he decided he would do the best he could with *this* life that he had caused to happen. Then, when Jason and I broke up, my dad told his dad, and then his dad told him, and then ..." She paused and smiled. "And then he didn't waste a second in coming over here and telling me all this. And everything was whole again. Until Jason's death."

Smith thought about what Beth had said. On the one hand, he had no question in his mind that if there was such a thing as soul mates, these two were that. He suddenly remembered what Ella had said about how much Beth reminded her of Gwen Gerber and how much Arthur was like Jack Hunter. *Hey, wasn't it Ella who had called them all old souls?* He got a sudden chill, like another déjà vu feeling, but he shook it off.

But also, feelings this intense, passions this strong—well, he'd seen them explode before. And that bit about Arthur waiting until he and Beth died to be together again—without the feeling that was in Beth's voice when she said it, and the look on her face, it might sound more obsessive than romantic. Arthur was still on the hook. Smith did have another question, though.

"You said you broke up with Jason before Arthur came to you and told you all this. You mentioned that the other day. Why *did* you break up with Jason, then?"

Beth hesitated. "I hate to say it about him. I don't want to hurt his mother any more than she's already been hurt. But after about five or six weeks of dating, Jason changed. He started acting very strangely. At first, it was just that it seemed like he was calling me every two minutes. Then, he didn't want me to do anything without him, or to see any other friends. I mentioned this to his mom once or twice. I began to be frightened of him, even though he never actually threatened to hurt me. When I resisted his behavior, he just said that something bad might happen."

"He never said what?"

"No. But still, I felt fear for myself. And I know how it works that, when you're dealing with someone whose pain and fear make him act this way, the safest thing is to get out of the situation before he becomes even more obsessed. It was all too much. But I was very clear that I cared about him—that we had been friends for so long, and I would always want only the best for him. That I wanted him to get help for his pain. He seemed to accept the breakup at first. But when he saw Arthur and me talking in town, I think he could tell that Arthur and I would be together again. And he wouldn't talk to me after that—he withdrew from everything. And that worried me."

"Is that when you went to see his mother?"

"Exactly! I was surprised that she didn't already know Jason and I broke up. It had been a couple of weeks already. She said she hadn't noticed anything different about him, and she didn't think I had anything to worry about. I asked her to talk to him at least—to ask him about it. She said she would."

Smith shook his head. So much detail, so sincere—Beth seemed to believe that everything she told him was the truth. However, he knew that the truth could be different for different people, and each could believe they were right. "I have to tell you that Mrs. Berger denies you told her you broke up with Jason."

Beth looked surprised, and then confused. "But why would she say that?"

"She said that, when you came to visit, it was just to say hello. She said that if you *had* broken up, there was no way Jason wouldn't have told her."

"I don't understand." Beth paused, shaking her head as she thought. "Maybe she feels guilty. Maybe, whatever happened to Jason, she feels like she could have prevented it if she had gone looking for him. So maybe the only way she can deal with her fear that this may be true is to forget the whole conversation, or to deny it."

Smith was struck by this explanation, and he felt another itch starting at the back of his brain. He also was struck by this level of understanding of human nature in someone so young. He prided himself on this type of understanding, but he hadn't once thought of the explanation that Beth had just considered. He allowed Beth to see this in his eyes, but he wasn't finished.

"One more question—was Richard there when you went to see Mrs. Berger?"

"Richard? No, he was in Boston then, wasn't he?"

Smith ignored the question. "So, no one else heard the conversation?"

"No. Someone may have seen me go there, but she doesn't deny that part. Why ... Oh, my goodness. You have to think there's a chance she's telling the truth, which would mean *I* was lying. But, you know, even though I didn't tell her how long ago I had broken up with Jason, or that Arthur and I were back together, other people knew—my dad, Arthur's dad—"

Smith shook his head slightly. Beth must have noticed and understood his thoughts. She looked up at Smith and smiled ironically.

"I know they're not exactly impartial," she continued, "but you can't think they'd lie about this. We weren't making it full public knowledge yet—about me and Arthur—so that it wouldn't be as hard for Jason. People would have thought it was the cause of the breakup. We decided to wait about a month. But some friends knew also."

"Good. Who?"

Beth sighed. "Well, there's Mary Louise, for one."

"At the library?"

"Yes, do you know her?"

"Not yet. You didn't tell Ella?"

"That Jason and I broke up, yes. But not that Arthur and I were back together. I felt bad not to, but she's in the same quilting circle as Kathy—as Mrs. Berger—and I didn't want Jason to find out yet, although he did say he expected it to happen someday."

"He did? When did he say that?"

"Right on our first date."

"I see." Smith thought for a moment. "Okay then, I guess that's all for now. I appreciate your opening up the way you did. If it helps you to know, I think you did help. Quite a bit." He pushed back in his chair and they both stood up.

Beth smiled. "I'm glad of that. Do you … Do you think there's hope?"

"I think there's more work to do, and I can't guarantee anything, but yes, I think we've made a good start."

"How exactly did I help?"

"I can't tell you that yet."

"I see. I understand."

Smith smiled, knowing that she thought he wasn't "at liberty" to tell her how she had helped, when really it was that it wasn't clear enough yet for him to explain it. He had to let everything percolate a little bit longer. And there was a new itch in the back of his brain that he had to scratch.

Chapter 21

Considering how many years Marie had lived alone before meeting Jeremy, it surprised her how much she missed him when they were apart for even a short while. She still enjoyed spending time alone occasionally, though. And she was very much enjoying her walk in town, looking at all the shops.

When she got to the bookstore, she opened the door and peered in.

"Marie!" said Tony. "Come on in."

"I've got the dogs," said Marie, apologetically. "I just wanted to say hello."

"Bring them. I'd like to meet them."

"Oh, great!" Marie walked through the door, her legs continuously being whacked by two oscillating dog tails.

"Oh, they're cute," said Tony. "What color is that?"

"It's called apricot."

"Oh. Anyway, it was nice to talk to you at the wedding. I hadn't realized you did white water rafting too, so it was fun to compare notes."

"Yes, it was."

"Where's Jeremy?"

Marie hesitated. "I think he's still helping Bob out with something."

Tony frowned. "I really can't believe what's been happening. And I still don't believe Arthur did this. He couldn't have. Jason had been acting like a jerk lately, but there's nothing he did that would make someone kill him, let alone Arthur."

Marie hesitated again, but couldn't restrain herself. "A jerk?" she said, casually. "You never mentioned that before. I didn't realize it."

"There was no reason to say anything when Jason's death was an accident. I can't imagine why they think it's anything else, and that Arthur, of all people, did it."

Marie ignored the questioning glance Tony was giving her, suddenly realizing that she wasn't the only one fishing for information. She decided she was over her head and should extricate herself from this conversation, though she'd be sure to tell Jeremy that Tony might have some information about Jason to confirm what David had told him.

"Anyway," she said, "it was nice to see you again. The dogs are getting antsy. I'd better get them outside and walking again."

"Okay, then." Tony looked disappointed for just a fleeting moment before his smile returned. "Thanks for stopping by. And say hi to Jeremy."

"I will. Take care."

Out on the street again, Marie took a deep breath, beginning to understand why it was so easy for news to spread in a small town. It was very tempting to talk to people you knew and liked. She and the dogs continued their walk.

Oh, a real estate office! Marie stopped to look. It seemed that every place they went on this trip, they thought about how nice it might be to live there, and they'd look at the listings in the window of a real estate agency.

The dogs began to pull on their leashes. "Chili wait! Sparky wait!" The dogs sat down and she continued to look, amazed at the range of home prices in the area—from small fixer-uppers in the low one hundred thousands to homes on waterfront acreage for half a million and more, and everything in between. There also seemed to be a few charmers—old farmhouses or craftsman-style homes that had been renovated—like the one Jeremy described that Beth's family owns.

"Can I help you with anything?"

Marie looked up. A very short, buxom woman with long, black hair was standing in the doorway of the office. She had a friendly smile on her face and seemed very warm and down-to-earth. She looked to be in her late thirties or early forties.

"Hi, no, thank you. I'm just looking for fun. My husband and I are in town for a wedding, and we like it here so much that I was curious."

"Oh, that must be Jenny Lynne's wedding."

Marie smiled. "Yes, that's right."

"I used to baby-sit for her. It's hard to believe she's married. You know, I think I did see you at the wedding. You're the wife of the policeman, aren't you? The one who's helping out with Jason's murder."

"Yes, that's me." Marie braced herself.

"That's a real heartbreaker! I used to baby-sit for him too after his father died, and for his cousin Richard when he moved in after *his* parents died. That family's seen more than its share of grief. I'm Eileen, by the way."

"It's nice to meet you. I think I did see you at the wedding also." Marie hesitated. Jeremy was always talking about wanting to know what the people in an investigation were really like, and Eileen seemed so approachable. Marie was tempted to ask her about it, and she finally gave in to the temptation. "I wonder what they were like as children—Jason and Richard, I mean."

"Oh, Jason was a sweetheart. Richard, on the other hand, was a selfish little boy. He seemed to want to take everything for himself and not share. It may have been just a reaction to losing his parents that way, though. He maybe felt insecure and like he didn't have anyone else on his side."

"I can see how he would."

"Yeah, I think that was it. But that would really set off the temper tantrums in Jason—when Richard would take something away from him. And Jason was the older one! Still, they made it through that time, God bless them. They became good friends to each other. And Richard can be a real charmer. I wasn't surprised when he left town, though. He never really had any other close friends—it was like he didn't want to make attachments here because he knew he was looking to find something different for himself."

"Well," said Marie, "I'm glad I got to meet you. If we ever decide to move here, I'll look you up."

"And I'll be happy to help you. Have a safe trip back."

"Thanks. Bye."

Eileen smiled and went back inside.

What a nice woman, thought Marie. *There's something about her that you trust and that warms your heart. There are a lot of nice people in this town!*

Taking a deep breath of very fresh air, she continued walking along the sidewalk with a light step and a smile on her face. Sparks, as usual, had his tail straight up, enjoying the new and strange smells. Chili Bean, as usual, had her tail down, still nervous in the unfamiliar surroundings, but still seeming, equally, to enjoy the smells.

Although Chili Bean was never as comfortable in an unfamiliar city as Sparks was, just let them loose on a trail in the forest and she took off, flying up and down, right and left, exploring everything. Sparks was happy to stay on the trail with the people most of the time.

As Marie approached Walker's Market, the door opened and a thin, angular woman who looked to be about ten years older than Marie walked out, accompanied by a young man.

"Oh," said the woman, "Poodles! How beautiful. What color is that?"

"Apricot," said Marie, with a smile. It was a common question.

The woman put her hand out and allowed Chili Bean to smell her fingers. Much to Marie's surprise, Sparks walked right up to her and sniffed her fingers as well. He was usually very cautious around strangers. Even more surprising, he allowed her to pet him without shying away.

"He likes you," said Marie. "He doesn't usually let strangers pet him right away."

The young man put his hand out, and sure enough, Sparks backed away. He turned to Chili Bean, but she backed away also. Surprisingly, though, she also growled. She never did that.

"Oh, I'm sorry," said Marie. "I think they must be more nervous with you because you're a man in a strange location."

"That's okay," said the young man, with a smile. Marie smiled back.

The woman looked at Marie. "With these two mini-poodles, you must be Jeremy Smith's wife."

Marie smiled. "Yes, I am."

"I'm Kathy Berger, and this my nephew, Richard."

Marie's face darkened. "Oh!" She instinctively placed her hand gently on Mrs. Berger's arm. "I'm so sorry for your loss. I can't even imagine."

"No, it seems nobody can." She looked down at the dogs. "But I have to thank you. I forgot for a moment—for the first time since … since it happened—when I saw your dogs."

"Aunt Kathy's a real dog person," said Richard. "She's always had a way with them."

Marie smiled. "Well, I'm glad if you got a moment of peace."

"Yes," said Mrs. Berger, her voice harsher now, and her words clipped, "but that's gone now. Good-bye. I hope you enjoy your visit."

This time, as they walked off, both Chili Bean and Sparks growled faintly.

Well, she thought, *Richard is definitely not a dog person if Chili Bean growled at him.* Despite the explanation she had given to make Richard feel less rejected, Chili Bean actually loved men. *But he did seem like a nice young man. I can see why Eileen called him a charmer.*

Marie looked at her watch and headed over to the observation deck that overlooked the river. Jeremy would be picking her up there soon. They'd go home for lunch, and then he'd be off again with Bob Penny. As she sat down on the bench, she wondered what he would say about the meeting she just had.

No, she knew what he would say. Just because someone didn't get along with dogs, it didn't mean they were "of interest to the police." And he would tell her about all the terrible people in the world who supposedly loved dogs and treated them well.

Still, she'd tell him anyway, of course. She liked Kathy Berger—she saw a sweetness in her, before she was reminded of her son's death. Suddenly, the case Jeremy was helping with had become much more personal to her. And despite Richard's charm, there was something out of the ordinary there if Chili Bean growled at him, I don't care what Jeremy says—especially thinking back to what Eileen had said about him.

"Hey!" The dogs suddenly went wild, barking and pulling on their leashes. Marie looked up. Jeremy was walking toward them. "Quiet! Sit! Sit!"

The dogs responded only halfheartedly until Jeremy reached them. As soon as he petted them, they resumed their good behavior.

"Hi, darlin'," said Smith.

Marie smiled. She loved how he called her that, but she never told him because she was afraid it would make him self-conscious about it and he would stop.

"Hi, honey."

They kissed.

"I took a parking spot up the block in case you weren't ready to go. Boy, you really seemed lost in thought."

Marie decided to jump right in. "I guess I was. I met Kathy Berger and Richard."

"How did that happen?"

"Need you ask? Small town, remember? Anyway, she loves dogs, apparently, and stopped to meet the kids. I guess she knew you had two mini-poodles, so she knew who I was and introduced herself and Richard."

"Oh."

"It was really strange. Sparks went up to her like he had known her forever. He really liked her. Chili Bean liked her too. But neither of them liked Richard at all. They both growled at him—even Chili."

"Now, Marie, just because someone doesn't get along with dogs, it didn't mean they're criminals. There are plenty of terrible people in the world who say they love dogs and treat them well."

Marie sighed. "I know. But …"

"But?"

"But I also met a lovely woman named Eileen who used to baby-sit for Richard and Jason—and Jenny, too!"

"Who is she?"

Marie hesitated. "She works at the real estate office."

"Real estate!"

"Just let me tell you! She said that Richard became kind of a bully after his parents died—that he was selfish."

"He doesn't come across that way."

"No, I know. Eileen said he grew out of it. But he used to bully *Jason* a lot is the point of it. I thought you might be interested in something that could shed some light on their relationship."

Smith paused in thought. "I am. Thanks. He bullied Jason, she said?"

"Yes."

"Well, it's something to keep in mind."

"Oh, and one more thing. Tony says Jason had been acting like a jerk lately, just like David told you, so maybe you or Bob could ask him about it."

Smith looked at Marie with a frown. "You've been busy, I see."

Marie ignored the frown. "Yes, I have. So, how did your talk with Beth go?"

"It was very interesting. Actually, I'm glad you're ready to go, because I have some thinking to do before Bob comes to get me. I wonder what kind of a morning he's having."

Chapter 22

Penny sat across the conference table from Jimmy Benson at the barracks. Jimmy was a good state trooper. He did solid work and didn't lose his head. Penny had been worried at first that Jimmy knew too many of the people involved in this case way too well to be objective, having grown up with them. Now, though, Penny was reminded of how grateful he always had been to have someone with Jimmy's knowledge to assist him.

"Here you go, Bob." Jimmy passed Penny a couple of folders.

"Thanks." Penny had decided to cross reference the names David had given him of people who had argued with Jason recently with the files they had on some of the young men in town. These were the matches. "Let's see. Okay, this one's interesting. I didn't know that Tommy had a record with us."

"Let me see," said Jimmy. "Oh yeah, you were away on vacation that week. It wasn't much of anything. Just too much to drink, and he got into it with someone at the pub—a pool game, I think."

"Yeah, that's what it says here."

"He can get nasty when he drinks, but he always sobers up remorseful. I've never known him to hold a grudge. I don't see him getting offended by Jason and planning revenge or anything."

"Go ahead and check out his alibi anyway. I'll check out the others myself." The phone rang, and Penny answered. He listened for a minute. "Great," he said, before he hung up.

"We got the warrant. They're faxing it over. I had my doubts, but the judge felt that it was suspicious enough—Richard being here and not telling us, and also the hammer not being found until the day after Jason died and Richard having access to Jason's hair."

"That's good news."

Penny glanced at the other files on his desk. "You're right, Jimmy, and so was David. None of this seems like much. I'll still talk to them—all but one of them, anyway. Pete Markowicj is gone. He moved to California with his whole family the day after the incident with Jason. According to David, it was actually at Pete's goodbye party that Jason took offense to a remark Pete made." The fax machine started up, and Penny got up and stood by it.

"What did Pete say?" asked Jimmy.

"The way David tells it, all he said was that Jason should come out and visit him in California, now that he was free to. That he wanted to show him hospitality. He probably was referring to Jason's breakup with Beth and saying it left Jason free. Apparently many people *had* noticed the breakup, by the way. But David thought Pete meant it in a nice way—that he was trying to say, 'Hey, buddy, good riddance,' to make him feel better. For some reason, Jason went ballistic. They had to pull him off of Pete."

"Strange."

"It is that." He picked up the papers that had just come in on the fax. "Well, I'm off to see Richard. I'll take this warrant with me, but I hope I don't need to use it. Maybe Richard will spare his aunt the stress and get the rental records for us. I'm stopping at Mary Louise's first to talk to her, so I'll be a while. I told Jeremy Smith I'd pick him up at one." He looked at his watch. "I hope I can make it. Hold down the fort."

"Right."

Mary Louise lived about ten minutes outside of town in the opposite direction from the Berger place. Penny pulled into her driveway and walked up to the front door. Paulie, her tow-headed, five-year-old son, opened the door before Penny could knock.

"Hi, Paulie."

"Hi, can I turn on your siren?"

Penny laughed. "Not right now, but maybe before I leave. Is your mom here?"

Mary Louise called out, "In the kitchen."

Penny followed Paulie in. His mother was standing by the sink, long brown hair tied up in a ponytail, drying her hands on a dishtowel. "Sorry. I had my hands in a wad of dough. I'm baking today. That was a great wedding yesterday, wasn't it? Jennie was beautiful. And Maggie looked great, too. She looks happy."

"Thanks. I'll tell her."

"I already did. So, what's up?"

"I just wanted to confirm something with you. What do you know about the status of Jason and Beth's relationship before he died, and about Beth and Arthur?"

Mary Louise frowned. "I hate thinking about this. It's crazy."

"I know. I wish I didn't have to talk about it either."

"Well, anyway, we have to, I guess. But there's not much to say. I know that she and Jason broke up about two weeks ago. Something had been bothering Beth for a couple of weeks before that, but she wouldn't say what. Then, she told Ella and me the morning after they broke up. She said it just wasn't working, and it was probably best that they go back to being friends."

"She didn't give any specifics about why they broke up?"

Mary Louise hesitated. "Not then. But about two days later, she came in like she was floating on a cloud—well, Beth's not the floating type, maybe, so more like she was lit up, like a Christmas tree—happy, you know."

"I get the picture."

"Later, when we were alone, she told me that Arthur came over when he heard she and Jason broke up and told her how sorry he was—that he realized how stupid he had been. She told me they were back together for good this time—oh, God, and look what happened! I still can't believe it. But anyway, she didn't want anyone to know for a month or so. She didn't want it to seem like she had broken up with Jason because of Arthur."

"Did you think it was strange that she should worry about that?"

"Not really. Beth has a very warm and caring heart. I guess I just thought she was protecting his ego. She even was going to let it slip around town that Jason broke up with her. But ..." Mary Louise seemed reluctant to continue.

"But?" Penny asked, encouragingly.

Mary Louise sighed. "But she also said something that made me wonder if it was Jason she was protecting or herself. She wasn't convinced that I understood how important it was that I not say anything about her and Arthur being back together. She normally would talk to Ella about this kind of thing, since Ella knows everyone so well and usually gives Beth pretty good advice. But this time, she told me she was afraid to tell her because Ella sees Jason's mom once a week. I don't know. It made it seem like she was more afraid about Jason finding out she was back with Arthur than about other people knowing."

"I see. And you're sure about the timing of all this?"

"Yes, I'm positive."

"Okay, then. Thanks for your help."

"Can you ... can you say hello to Arthur from us?"

"I'll do that today. Thanks again." Penny turned toward the door and almost tripped over Paulie, who had been right behind him.

"Now? Can I do the siren now?"

"Paulie, leave Bob alone. And it makes too much noise. It's Sunday!"

Penny looked down at Paulie's crestfallen face and weakened. Smiling inside, but keeping his face very serious, he said, "Well, how about just the lights. And you can talk to Jimmy on the radio."

*****

Twenty minutes later, Penny pulled onto the Berger property. During the drive over here, his grumpiness had resurfaced. He had decided that it was his job to get to the bottom of all this, and he wasn't going to worry about hurting anyone's feelings anymore. If Richard didn't cooperate, he was just going to shove the warrant in his face and get on with it. He knocked on the door and waited.

"Just a minute." It was Richard's voice. He opened the door. "Oh, Bob. Is there news?"

"Not the news your aunt is waiting for yet. I need to talk to you, though. Are you alone?"

"Yes. Aunt Kathy's out in the field. What is it?"

"I need to see the records of your house rental. Do you know where she keeps them?"

"What! Why in the world would you need to see that?"

"Well, it turns out that we do have independent corroboration that not only did your cousin and Beth break up a couple of weeks ago, but she was back with Arthur a few days afterward. This weakens the motive quite a bit, so we're looking to see if we can find another reason they may have argued. I'm assuming that, when you said your aunt managed your rental for you, you meant they both did—she and Jason. I'd guess it was maybe more Jason that did the actual work. She mentioned that she didn't feel confident to manage the farm alone."

"Well, maybe he did do the books. Sometimes he would fix a few things for me, and charge me for his time.

But it's my aunt who communicates with me about things. And I still don't see—"

"With you mentioning how you've had a lot of tenants, we just want to see if there's a connection between any of your tenants and Arthur, or maybe a connection with Jason—some bad feeling that built up."

"I don't see how—oh, if it *weren't* Arthur, you mean, then maybe an old tenant who was angry could have killed him. But I don't see the connection to Arthur. And I'm not sure I want to show you anything without talking to a lawyer."

Penny sighed and reached into his back pocket. "I have a warrant, Richard. Just get me the records."

Richard frowned, and took the papers Penny held out. He looked them over quickly.

"I hope you know where they are," said Penny. "I'd hate to bother your aunt with all of this right now, bringing her back here from her work, worrying her—"

"Okay, then. Enough. I know where the books are." Richard walked into the kitchen. Penny followed.

"Here." Richard handed Penny two books that he retrieved from a drawer.

"Thank you." Penny glanced through the books. The first was a ledger of payments and expenses. The other was a narrative. It listed tenant names and phone numbers, references—that kind of thing. Penny was happy to see that it also listed forwarding addresses for after they moved. He flipped through a few pages, and then stopped. Keeping his face impassive, he looked up at Richard.

"I'll need to take these for a short while."

"Take them! But—"

Penny held his hand up. "Yes, but just for a short while. I'll give you a receipt."

"We need them back."

"Of course. Thanks for your cooperation, Richard. I'll get them back to you as soon as I can."

Penny got out of the house as fast as he could, sat down in his car, and opened the book again.

Markowicj. *Now, that's very interesting.*

He got on the radio. "Hey, Jimmy, I have a question. Ron Markowicj—that's Pete's big brother, isn't it."

"Yeah, why?"

"Do you know if he moved with the family?"

"No, his wife didn't want to leave her parents. They live up near them now, about an hour north of here."

"I'm thinking he might have been down here for the goodbye party."

"That's a good guess."

"I have a phone number for you. Check and see if it's still good. And see if you can get an address. I'll be right in."

Penny looked at his watch, which read 10:15 AM.

Let's see, if I leave at ten-thirty, an hour up and back, and at least a half-hour there—that's cutting it too close. Jeremy may have to go to see Arthur on his own.

*****

It took ten minutes to get back to the barracks. Jimmy was just hanging up the phone when he got there.

"What did you get?" asked Penny.

"We're in luck. Ron works construction. He's on a site that's just about half an hour away."

"Great. Give me the info, and I'm off."

Jimmy handed him a piece of paper.

"Oh," said Penny. "Hold on." He flipped through the rental books. "Well, it looks like Ron and his wife rented Richard's house for six months. I don't see anything to show if there were problems—late payments, problems with repairs. Look, Jimmy, while I'm gone, start checking through these books. Write out a list of tenants' names for me and when and how long they rented. Also, see if you can figure out if there's anything in the books that indicates problems—anything unusual."

"Will do."

Penny returned to his car and headed back in the same direction as the Berger place. He passed the turnoff to their house and kept going north. He wasn't sure whether this would amount to anything or not. He couldn't ignore the double connection, of course—Ron having been the last tenant in Richard's house and his younger brother being one of the people who had a run-in with Jason. But was it plausible to think that Ron stole Arthur's hammer to kill Jason? What reason could there be to plan something like that, and to be willing to frame someone else for it? No, a fight that got out of hand—that would make more sense.

After another fifteen minutes or so, Penny made a right turn onto a narrow road—it was more like a driveway, but it had a street sign. Another five minutes, and Penny was at the site. There was a big backhoe in operation. It looked like they were digging a foundation for a house. He walked up to the nearest man.

"Is Ron Markowicj around?"

The man pointed to a group of workers who were unloading piles of something from a flatbed truck. Squinting, Penny recognized that they were the forms that would be assembled in the foundation of the building to receive the cement.

"Thanks." Penny approached the group of men.

"Ron Markowicj?"

"Yeah. It's Bob Penny, isn't it? My wife called. What can I do for you?"

Penny gestured, and the two men walked off to the side.

"I don't know if you heard about Jason Berger …"

Markowicj frowned. "What about him?"

"He died a couple of days ago."

Markowicj's eyes widened in surprise. "Did he have a heart attack, or did someone finally have enough of him?"

Penny didn't know what to make of this reaction. The surprise seemed spontaneous, but there certainly wasn't any sadness in it.

"It seems like it would be the latter."

Markowicj looked uncomfortable. "Well, what does it have to do with me?"

"We're talking to everyone who had recent contact with Jason, to try to get a picture of his frame of mind. You were the last tenant renting from him—"

"I rented from Richard."

"But I guess you dealt with Jason also. And then you saw him at your brother's goodbye party."

Markowicj sighed. "Look, I guess I just let it slip that I didn't care much for the guy, but I didn't wish him dead or anything—I was a little out of line there with that comment. He was a friend of my brother. I never had a problem with him until I rented that house."

"What problem was that?"

"I work construction. It's seasonal, *you* know that. Mrs. Berger knew that too. When I rented the place, I asked about it—about maybe being late with the rent in the winter once in a while. She said as long as I eventually paid up and it wasn't every month, it would be okay—if it just happened once in a while in the winter. Then, the first month that I have to be late, Jason shows up. He was acting like a jerk. He said if I didn't come up with the money by the next day, I had thirty days to get out—he'd evict us. It was crazy. I told him what his mother had said, and he knew I was Pete's brother. I never saw that side of him before. It's like he took it personal—like I was disrespecting him or something."

"What did you do?"

"I called his mother and told her what happened. I reminded her of what she'd said. She was apologetic, but she said she wouldn't go against what her son said. I told them to forget it—we'd be out in a week, and screw their money. We moved in with my wife's parents until we found another place."

"And this was in January?"

Markowicj thought for a minute. "Almost into February."

Still, thought Penny, *it was well before Jason even started seeing Beth, let alone her breaking up with him. That can't explain his attitude.*

"You were still responsible to pay for the time you were there, you know."

"I know, I know. My wife made me send them two weeks rent."

"So, how was it when you saw Jason at the party? I'm surprised your brother invited him."

"They were still friends, though. My brother, I have the idea, maybe thought I had exaggerated—that my temper had partially caused the problem. But lately, I'm told that other people started to see the side of Jason that I saw. When he acted like a jerk at the party, I think Pete realized that maybe I *hadn't* exaggerated. Pete just made some kind of comment to Jason about hospitality and Jason went crazy. We had to pull him off."

It didn't slip by Penny's attention that Markowicj had said he had a temper. "What happened after that?"

"Nothing. He left. We didn't say anything about my history with him or anything. Everyone just thought he was overly sensitive because of the breakup with Beth. I have to say, I don't know what she saw in him to begin with. She's a really nice girl. She has a heart of gold. Maybe Arthur will get off his duff and try to get her back. I don't know how he let her get away."

Penny didn't address this last comment, but it seemed that Ron didn't even know that Arthur was in jail, let alone, maybe, his having been the one to put him there. But this gave Penny another line of inquiry. He had to be sure.

"Do you know Arthur well?"

"Better than Jason. He's a good guy. He and my youngest brother, Mitch, were very tight in school, so I saw a lot of Beth then also. If she and Arthur weren't obviously made for each other, I might have had a go at her myself. Don't tell my wife I said that!"

Penny couldn't hide his smile.

"And where were you on Thursday? Here?"

"Is that when he died? No, I was on another site, about an hour north of here. They weren't ready for us here yet. They're still digging now—finishing up. But we got really behind, with all that rain we had two weeks ago, so they have us here today to get started. The backhoe will be done by lunchtime."

"And you didn't hold a grudge against Jason?"

"For what. He did me a favor. We have a much nicer place. With my parents and my brother gone, we get to be closer to my wife's family. My job wasn't affected. I just didn't like the guy much. Like I said, I didn't wish him dead. His mother's a sweetheart also, even if she turned out to be weak where her son was concerned."

"You may not have wished it on him, but you didn't sound very sad that he *was* dead."

"What I said before, when you told me he died—I only meant that, with how he was acting, he could have worked himself up into a heart attack, or really pissed off the wrong person. I was being a smart ass. If I had really thought about it, I would have assumed he had died in an accident or something."

"Well, you've been helpful. It gives us a clearer picture of him. Are you going to be around the next few days?"

"I'll be here."

"And who can I talk to, just to confirm where you were Thursday? It's routine."

"Anyone." He waved his hand. "The contactor on this job is different, but …" He looked around and then pointed. "There, the site manager knows. And three of the guys here today were with me at that site also." He pointed again.

"You were there all day?"

"Yeah. No place to go for lunch. I was there from 7:00 AM to 4:00 PM."

"Okay, then. Thanks for your help."

"No problem."

Penny took the time to verify Markowicj's alibi on Thursday, and then headed back. It didn't look like he had turned up anything specific, but Markowicj did confirm that there was another side to Jason that preceded his sadness at losing Beth—a side that Beth had hinted at as well. And there could be other tenants that Jason screwed around with who were still upset.

Or, if Richard found out about this, he could have been *very* upset. He was worried enough about it to sneak down here and check things out. If he thought Jason was costing him tenants, how might he react?

Penny looked at his watch. He'd be getting back to the barracks at around twelve-thirty. There'd be time for him to grab a bite to eat before he picked up Jeremy.

Chapter 23

Jimmy pushed away the remnants of the pizza he had shared for lunch with Penny, opened one of the ledgers, and sighed. This wasn't his favorite part of the job. He was more of a people person. But he knew it had to be done. Investigator Penny had been clear about that before he left to pick up Jeremy Smith. And anyway, now Penny wanted him to contact some of the tenants himself, which would be more interesting.

This first book was fairly straightforward. It had the names of tenants, their background information and references, and all of their contact information—standard stuff for a rental. He made a simple list with names, possible phone numbers—family, personal references, jobs, etc.—and the dates that each tenant occupied the house. Looking back, he did notice that, over the last two years, there had been several tenants. Before that, one tenant had stayed for five years.

Then he opened the second book, and this is when he groaned. It was divided into two parts. The first part was a standard set of books showing income—as in rent—and expenses. He didn't know what he could make of that. *Hey, maybe Marie could look at it for us.*

The last section of the book was more interesting. It seemed to have notes and comments about the rentals. *This might have something—*

Just then, the radio came on. It was one of the dispatchers.

"Hi, Sally, what do you have?"

"We have a fender bender in the Walker's parking lot in town. You're obviously the closest, if you're available."

"That's affirmative."

"One car left the scene. The other car and some witnesses are waiting for you."

"I'm on my way."

Jimmy closed the books and locked them up in a cabinet. Then he headed out. When he pulled into the parking lot at the supermarket, he saw a small crowd at the far end, near the back driveway. He pulled close and parked. As he approached the group, a woman walked up to him. She looked a little shaken.

"Hello, Officer. I'm glad you're here. I was in my car, parked in a regular spot, and someone just bashed right into me like I wasn't even there. He pushed me out into the lane. I'm lucky no one else hit me."

"Are you sure you're okay?" said Jimmy. "Should I call an ambulance?"

"No, I'm fine. Just a little shook up."

"Then, I'll need to see your license and registration." She fumbled in her purse and handed it to him. He noted that she had a New York City address. "You said 'he.' Did you see the person in the car?"

"No. I didn't even see the car, really. It was a light color is all I can say. But there are a couple of witnesses." She pointed to the group standing behind her. Two men walked forward. Jimmy didn't know either of them, but he recognized one as being local.

"I saw the whole thing," said the local man. "It was one of the guys that I see going into the Bait and Tackle shop a lot. I don't know his name, but if you describe him and the car, Clay will know who it is."

"I actually got the license plate number," said the other man, "but I didn't see who was driving."

"It was that guy," said the first man, "and it was the car he always drives."

"Okay, then," said Jimmy. "I'll take both your names and phone numbers, and that license plate number. And ma'am, I really think you should consider letting someone take a look at you."

"No, I'm fine, thank you. Maybe you can just wait and make sure I can drive my car."

It was determined that she could. Jimmy watched her leave as the crowd dispersed.

Getting back in his patrol car, Jimmy was about to drive to Clay's Bait and Tackle when he remembered that Tommy worked at Walkers. *I'm here. I might as well talk to him now.* He radioed in to run the license plate information and went inside the store. Mary, the manager, was up front.

"Hi, Mary, is Tommy around?"

"He's in back, doing the order for the meat department. Do you want me to call him out, or can you find your way?"

"I'll find my way, thanks."

In back, Jimmy was happy to find Tommy alone. "Hey, Tommy, can I talk with you for a minute?"

A thin, redheaded young man of medium height looked up from the notebook he was reading. "Oh, hi, Jimmy. Sure. What's up?"

Jimmy noted that Tommy looked happy to see him. He didn't have a suspicious or nervous look about him at all. "I'm just checking up on Jason Berger's death, you know, and we're trying to get an idea of his state of mind. We hear that he'd been acting like he was upset for a while there."

Tommy's face darkened. "That he was, but it's still a sad thing, what happened to him. I had a run-in with him a couple of weeks ago myself." He smiled. "I guess you must know that, if you're here. Anyway, he came into the pub, and all I did was ask him, 'Where's Beth?' and he turned all red and swung at me."

"That's all you said?"

"That's it. I hadn't even heard they broke up. I was just asking. So, anyway, a couple of guys grabbed his arms and walked him out, and that was it."

"You didn't see him after that?"

"Nope."

"And can you tell me what you were doing on Thursday afternoon?"

"That's the day Jason died, I know." He thought for a minute. "I was here until seven. I had my break at two, and I hung out with Joyce the whole time, except maybe for a quick trip to use the facilities. She's off today, but Mary can vouch for most of it, and you can catch Joyce at home if you need to, or she'll be here tomorrow. After work, I went straight home. My mother was there already."

"Right. Thanks, Tommy. It's just routine. And can you tell me who else was at the bar that night?"

Tommy gave him the names of the two men who escorted Jason to the door. "He had quieted down by then, though," said Tommy. "He even apologized."

"Okay then. I'll check it out. Thanks again."

Jimmy went back to his patrol car and looked at his watch. *I guess I need to get moving on this guy who left the accident scene.* He'd call in to see if they had the name of the owner of the car yet, and then he'd go talk to Clay and see if he had a name also. Hopefully, the two names would match.

This definitely was slowing down his review of the ledgers on Richard's rental. If he didn't get back to it today, he knew he'd need to come in tomorrow, day off or not. There wasn't anyone else. August was always short because of vacations.

But Penny had also been very clear about what Senior Investigator Jacobs had said—their regular work was to come before any more investigating on Jason's murder—so the ledgers would have to wait.

Chapter 24

"I agree." Penny kept his eyes on the road as he spoke. "One of them is lying. That has to mean something."

Smith sighed. "Probably. But, Bob, you know as well as I do that people sometimes lie for reasons not related to the case. I thought Beth's insight was a good one about why Mrs. Berger might not be telling the whole truth. But if Beth is the one lying, there's no other reason than to protect Arthur." Smith smiled. "Oh, and Marie ran into Kathy Berger and Richard in town. She wanted us to know that the dogs really liked Kathy and hated Richard."

Penny laughed.

"Don't laugh. Those dogs are smart! But there's more. Tony told Marie that Jason had been acting like a jerk lately, just like David said, so you might want to talk to him also."

"He's already on my list."

"Good. And someone named Eileen used to baby-sit Jason and Richard and told Marie that Richard bullied Jason when they were kids."

"Eileen at the real estate office?"

"Yes, that's right."

Penny laughed. "Boy, even Marie's on the case!"

Smith laughed also. "She seems to manage that once in a while. It's interesting information, though."

"Yes, it is. I never saw that in Richard, but kids do grow up and change. It's definitely something to keep in mind. Hold on." Penny was quiet for a minute as he navigated onto the highway. "But what you said before," he continued, "I was thinking that maybe it's Beth who feels guilty—maybe she *meant* to tell Mrs. Berger she was worried about Jason but she didn't, so maybe she's so upset that she didn't warn Mrs. Berger that *she* blocked it out with a false memory."

Smith laughed. "Okay, I see your point, but I don't think so. The person that seems the most clearheaded and the least like they're hiding anything is Beth. Part of the problem, you know, is that it's hard to compare their demeanors. Mrs. Berger's grief could be altering her behavior, making her seem less believable, and Beth's love for Arthur could give her the strength to deceive us. But we know that one of them isn't telling the truth. That makes it seem like it must be either Arthur or Richard who did it, rather than someone we don't know about yet. Especially since it seems like Markowicj is out. That could have been promising."

"I know! But if it comes down to the lying, the DA's much more likely to believe the mother of the victim than the girlfriend of the man whose fingerprints are on the murder weapon."

"I can understand that. But now we know from other sources that Beth and Jason *did* break up, even if we don't know that Beth actually told Mrs. Berger. She wouldn't need to lie about that to protect Arthur. And we know from your talk with Mary Louise that Beth and Arthur were probably back together."

"And I still haven't given up on Markowicj or one of the other tenants, or on Richard being mad at Jason about how his tenants were being treated—if he found that out. I asked Jimmy to call some of the other ex-tenants this afternoon. Hopefully, he'll have the time."

"And the other guys David told you about?"

"Jimmy will have a talk with Tommy McPhee, and I'll talk with the rest later. But I'm also thinking that, if Beth told Arthur something about Jason—something, maybe, like what she told you about how Jason treated her—*that* could have led to a confrontation as well. Maybe we have a motive after all, and Arthur and Beth are just better actors than we knew."

"I see that, of course," said Smith. "But still, I can't get past the feeling that, if Mrs. Berger lied, there must be a reason. And that leads me to Richard."

"Unless, maybe there's some reason Beth needed us to think that Mrs. Berger, specifically, knew—exactly because she didn't."

"But how would that help Arthur?"

"I don't know. You know, Jeremy, we're not going to get past this evidence very easily. This isn't just one person's word against another's. If it were, Arthur would win hands down over Richard—maybe unfairly so. But the hammer and the situation between Arthur, Jason, and Beth—that's probably enough for the DA. It's only because we didn't find the hammer when we searched the first day that he isn't stopping my investigation. If, during the trial, it appears like there's a possibility that someone framed Arthur, the defense can use that, and the DA needs to be able to say we looked into it."

"I know."

"God, it's still that hammer that drives me crazy, even when everything else I eliminate seems to make the case against Arthur stronger."

Smith glanced at Penny, then turned his head to stare out his window. He could feel that itch getting stronger and stronger.

Smith and Penny were quiet for the rest of the trip. In Mountlake, Penny drove a few blocks past the state police building and pulled into the parking lot of the county correctional facility, a three-story, concrete building with portholes for windows. They entered through a metal detector, and Smith followed Penny through electric doors that a guard opened for them and down a long hallway.

"I already arranged for you to talk to Arthur, but it has to be in the interview room. The conversation will be recorded, and I'll be observing from behind a two-way mirror with someone from the DA's office. The DA's exact words were, 'Smith can't have it both ways. If he's assisting the police, he can't also use his connection with the Lynne's to call himself a friend of the family.'"

Smith smiled at Penny's change of voice when he quoted the DA, thinking that Maggie's acting ability must be rubbing off on him. "That's fine."

"Here you go," said Penny. There was a deputy sheriff standing outside a solid, grey door. At Penny's nod, he unlocked the door.

When Smith entered the room, Arthur was already waiting for him. He looked glum, like he had given up hope.

"Hello, Arthur, how are you doing?"

"Hi. Not so good, I guess."

"Mary Louise said to say shes thinking of you, and Mr. White sends his regards. He said to tell you he's praying for you."

Arthur's eyes watered. He sighed and sat up straighter. "Tell him thank you for me."

"I will. And Beth sends her love, of course."

Arthur winced, but there were no tears this time. He held his face steady and nodded, but his eyes revealed a pain as intense as the one Smith had seen in Beth's eyes. It was a type of pain that Smith could remember from when he looked in the mirror after his parents and his brother had died, one after the other.

"I see how much the two of you love each other. Beth made it very clear as well. How did this all happen then?"

"Because I'm an idiot, I guess." Arthur's face was filled with an anger that Smith knew he was directing at himself. "I don't know how to explain it ... I just felt like I couldn't deal with the pain of losing her if we stayed together. It was like it was something I had already experienced and couldn't bear to go through again. Like—I know! Kind of like my friend, Mitch. When we were little kids, he threw up on a roller coaster. The next year, his dad talked him into trying it again. As soon as it started to move, Pete started screaming to let him off—that he changed his mind. The difference for me is that I should have been able to keep in mind what I would be giving up, and to know that it would be worth it in the end to stay."

"But you did realize that eventually?"

"Yes, but I thought it was too late. Beth had already started seeing Jason. I had to accept that I had made a monumental mistake. I know how to accept responsibility for my own mistakes. I wasn't about to interfere in Beth's life again, and in Jason's. But then, when my dad told me they had broken up, I knew I was being given another chance. And believe me, I took it. I was over there in under a minute, it seemed like. Her parents were happy to see me, even though I had hurt their daughter so much. They seemed to know I had hurt myself just as much."

"And Beth?"

"And Beth ..." His voice choked up. "Beth understood. I don't know why, but she did. And she took me back into her life."

"So, you two were a couple again—what was it, about two weeks before Jason died?"

Arthur hesitated a moment, his eyes rising up and to the right as he thought—a sign to Smith that he probably would be telling the truth. "Maybe a little less. Maybe just twelve days or so."

"Did anyone but your and Beth's parents know?"

"Well, Jason did, if that's what you're asking. I'm not going to lie—about that or anything else. He saw us talking together and he could tell. I saw it in his eyes. But that was just a couple of days before he died. Oh, and Marie told a couple of her friends."

"Did *you* tell anyone?"

"Marie asked me not to. She wanted to wait a full month before people knew about us."

Smith decided to switch gears. "Tell me about the hammer."

"What about it? It's mine."

"Where did you keep it? When did you last see it? That kind of thing."

Arthur sighed. "I already told the police. I keep my toolbox in a shed on my parents' property. We don't lock it. And I don't *remember* the last time I saw it." He paused again, thinking. "I know it wasn't that long ago—maybe a couple of weeks."

There went Smith's idea that Jason might have got hold of it at Beth's house. "You don't remember ever lending it to anyone?"

"I don't know about *ever*, but not recently."

This time Smith sighed. This boy is not helping himself at all. Still, he was showing his honesty. And the shed wasn't locked, there *was* that.

"I do tell all my friends they can stop by and borrow anything they need," said Arthur, as if he had read Smith's mind, "but who'd come all that way just to borrow a hammer?"

So much for Arthur helping himself. Smith gave it one more try.

"So a lot people know you don't lock the shed, then?"

Arthur nodded.

Smith sighed. There was one more thing he needed to do in this interview.

"I guess Beth told you about how Jason was acting toward her—about why she broke up with him?"

Arthur looked uncomfortable for the first time in Smith's experience. Not angry so much as troubled.

"Yes."

"Did that bother you or worry you? Did you discuss it with Jason?"

"No. Beth had kept good feelings between them, even with the breakup. I got the feeling that he was more sad than angry. Until …"

"Until?"

Arthur sighed. "When Jason saw us in town and could tell we were together again, I did think he looked angry for a minute. And he stopped talking to Beth and me—when he ran into each of us separately in town the next day, he avoided us. But he didn't confront us in any way."

"You never spoke to him about it?"

"I was hoping I wouldn't have to—that he would work it out. But I would have, if it became necessary." Arthur looked right into Smith's eyes when he said this.

"I see. Well, thank you for talking to me, Arthur. I don't know what to tell you, except that neither Bob nor I think we know all there is to know about this, and we're still looking for the full story."

"I appreciate that."

When Smith walked out the door, Penny was standing on the other side, waiting for him. "So?"

"So," said Smith, "one thought we both had before was that, if Beth was right to be afraid of Jason, Jason could have done something threatening, especially after he saw them together. I wanted to see if I could pick up anything about that. And it definitely seemed to be a topic that shook up Arthur's nice-guy persona."

"I don't know if we can make anything out of what he said, but the Assistant DA seemed to like it."

"And also, I wanted to talk to Arthur myself before I thought too much more about things, to confirm the timing and to be sure of his feelings for Beth, which I am now. He doesn't seem obsessed. I believe what Beth and Arthur tell me—they give the same story but not exactly the same way. It doesn't sound rehearsed. And since we can check with other people who knew they were back together, we can be pretty sure of that part. It does weaken his motive. And Beth said that Jason felt all along that she'd be back with Arthur some day, so why would he be surprised by it?"

"She did, huh. That's interesting."

"I also had thought that maybe there was some way that Jason had the hammer with him already, and someone other than Arthur used it as a weapon of opportunity. That seems unlikely now, although the tool shed wasn't locked. But there's something else I can't put my finger on—something we haven't looked at."

"Well, let's see what information Jimmy has dug up and we'll go from there."

Chapter 25

Smith, Marie, and Penny sat in the coffee house in town, drinking espresso. Smith had called Marie from Mountlake, and they all had decided that she would meet them there. They found a quiet table away from other people.

"So, is there still a chance that Arthur is being framed, or not?" asked Marie. "It doesn't sound like you guys got much further today. Except, Jeremy, that after talking to Arthur, you still feel like he didn't do it."

"If he were being framed," said Penny, "we'd be back to Richard, wouldn't we, if it was after the fact. I can see how Richard might be able to get some of Jason's hair. He has a key to the Berger's house. He knows where Jason's room is. But the blood—I don't know about that. That's the main problem I have with the 'framing Arthur' theory, unless Jason or someone else got that hammer out of Arthur's tool shed beforehand and it *is* the murder weapon, and we just missed it on the first search."

"I guess so," said Smith, "except maybe—" Smith stopped short. The itch was gone. He knew what they had been missing all along.

"I know that look on his face," said Marie. "He just scratched an itch. The coffee's percolated."

Penny laughed. "What are you thinking, Jeremy?"

"We've been making an assumption, and that assumption has kept us from considering another possibility. We've been assuming that the person who framed Arthur, if he was framed, was also the one who murdered Jason. But what if one person murdered Jason, and someone else planted the hammer. Or, even if the same person planted the hammer, it occurred to me that we only have alibis for the time of Jason's death. Maybe we need to ask what people were doing after his death and before the hammer was found?"

"That would mean anyone, really, could have killed him," Marie said. "Tying someone to the hammer wouldn't help you. But haven't you already thought about that—if Arthur was framed, anyone could be the killer?"

"Actually," said Smith, "it means more than that."

"Yes," said Penny. "It also means that if someone knew that Jason was murdered by someone else, they might have implicated Arthur after the fact to protect that person, unless it's just a coincidence that Jason did have Arthur's hammer with him already. So looking at who had access to Jason's hair and to the hammer won't necessarily give us the actual killer, although it could point the way."

"I just don't see how someone could do that," said Marie. "How could someone frame someone else for a murder? I mean, it's bad enough if someone murders someone anyway, but to frame someone else! Why not just make it look like an accident."

Smith was quiet for a moment. There was another possibility that hadn't been mentioned, but he decided not to bring that up right now. He'd talk to Penny about it later.

"I know how you feel," said Smith. "But people do think sometimes that their best defense is to point a finger elsewhere. So, if someone planned to kill Jason and frame Arthur, they might have stolen the hammer beforehand. But whether they planned ahead to kill him or not, the idea to frame Arthur could have come later. And if you remember, even though Bob *did* think it was an accident at first, there was some evidence to make him question that even before the hammer was found. I wonder who might have known that, by the way, Bob—that you had questions?"

"I'm—"

Smith held up his hand, stopping Penny from continuing. Marie and Penny turned to follow his gaze. Mrs. Berger had just come into the coffee house. She saw them and walked over, nodding at Marie.

"Well, Bob, is there anything new? Do you know when the trial will be?"

"Not yet. The hearing's tomorrow. Do you want to sit down?"

"No, thank you. I think I'd like to be by myself for a while. I'm just in town to see my attorney. There's some business that needs to get done, about the farm and such."

It seemed to Smith that Mrs. Berger was softer, somehow, than she had been before—quieter, more subdued.

"I'm just going to get a cup of coffee to take home with me. Richard's over working on his own house, and it doesn't …" Her voice choked up for a moment, but she continued. "It doesn't seem to make sense to make a pot for just one person."

"Maybe it would be good for you to have some company," said Marie.

"No. Thank you, though." She moved over to the counter.

Smith looked over at Marie, who was looking very sad. She was always affected by other people's emotions, even feeling compassion toward someone who hadn't made the best choices in life. She was like Smith in that way, except that Smith had no qualms about seeing to it that people were held responsible for their choices, even when he felt compassion for them.

Marie and Penny, Smith noticed, were looking over his shoulder toward the counter. He turned his head. Mrs. Berger was fumbling with her wallet.

"I don't seem to … I guess I don't have … I thought I had …" She started to cry, quietly.

Marie jumped up and went to her, putting her arm around her shoulders. She brought her back to the table. Mrs. Berger sat down and sighed. She accepted a tissue from Marie.

"I'm sorry. I seem to be having some financial problems, but it may just be that I don't understand something. Jason took care of the books after Richard's father died—he was my husband's brother-in-law and took care of the books after my husband Tom died. I probably should have taken the time to learn it all then, but it's hard to have to worry about that kind of thing when you're grieving. My husband and I loved each other very much. It wasn't an easy time." She winced. "I thought I'd seen the last of that kind of pain. I never would have thought …"

"You know," said Marie, "I don't want to seem forward, but I'm a financial planner. I'd be happy to stop by and go over things with you. Maybe I could help."

"Oh, I don't think … I mean—"

"There wouldn't be a charge or anything," said Marie, quickly. "And you could check with the Lynne's if you want a reference first."

Penny looked over at Smith in amazement. Smith just smiled and shrugged his shoulders.

"Well, you know, thank you. I think I *will* accept your offer. A woman financial planner, my goodness. I was never good at math or science. Thank you. Would this evening be good for you, or tomorrow after lunch?"

Marie looked over at Smith, who nodded.

"Yes," said Marie. "Tomorrow after lunch will be fine. We're having dinner with the Lynne's tonight."

"I'll drop you off," said Smith. "I know where Mrs. Berger lives. Then I can pick you up in, say, two hours. Would that be enough time?"

"That should do it. I can call you if we need more time, if you go back to the RV. Can we make it one o'clock then, Mrs. Berger?"

"Yes, and it's Kathy. Thank you. You're very kind. I think I'll be going now."

"Can I get you that cup of coffee?" asked Smith.

"Oh, no, I guess I'll make some at home after all. I think I mostly just wanted to delay going home to the empty house—a break from it, you know. And I've certainly had that. One o'clock tomorrow then."

Marie nodded.

Mrs. Berger stood up, managed a smile around to everyone, and left the shop.

"Do you think it's a good idea for Marie to get involved with Kathy Berger right now?" asked Penny.

"Actually, I was thinking it would give me an opportunity to talk to her, when I pick Marie up. And you have the morning before Arthur's hearing to look into Richard's tenants and maybe get more corroboration that Beth and Arthur were back together."

"And I still have to talk to some of the people David mentioned at the wedding. I called Jimmy from Mountlake. There's a lot of tenant information to go through, and he had to check up on a fender bender this afternoon, so he couldn't get through it all. He's going to come in tomorrow morning and finish it up—he's supposed to be off tomorrow, but we know what *that's* like. Oh, also, he spoke with Tommy McPhee. His alibi's solid, and the argument with Jason didn't amount to much."

"You didn't think it would anyway."

"I know. But I want to talk to the rest of the local boys myself tomorrow. And I'll look into everybody's whereabouts *after* Jason died. Once we had that hammer, we never looked further into alibis—certainly not for the period of time after the body was found and before you found the hammer."

"I don't think I'm comfortable with trying to get any information from Kathy," said Marie. "I just want to do what I offered—help her."

"That's fine," said Smith. "I wouldn't ask you to. You do your thing, and when I come to get you, just help me to get a conversation going with her."

Marie hesitated for a minute, looking Smith in the eye. "Okay," she said, finally. "I can do that."

"Good," said Penny. "Then we're all set." He pushed back in his chair. "I don't know about you guys, but it's four-thirty on a Sunday, and I was supposed to be off today. I'm going home."

Chapter 26

"This place is lovely," said Marie.

"Yes," said Barbara. "There's no view of the river, but it's a pretty room, the food's good, and the people are wonderful."

"The people seem great everywhere around here," said Smith. "I think it's a special place."

Barbara and Allan both smiled. "Yes," said Allan, "it is that."

"It seems like you would fit right in," said Barbara. "That was kind of you to offer to help Kathy with her money situation."

Marie looked surprised. "How did you know about that?"

"Oh, Kathy called and told me. I think she wanted me to vouch for you. I was happy to do it."

"I'm glad she reassured herself," said Marie. "It will make it easier for me to help her tomorrow. I wouldn't have mentioned it to you myself because of confidentiality, but since *she* did, that's okay."

"Actually," said Allan, "Barbara and I were wondering if there weren't more to this than helping Kathy. Are you using Marie as your inside man, by any chance, Jeremy?"

Smith laughed. "No, this was all Marie's heart at work."

"But after what you went through in England last year, Marie," said Barbara, "trying to find your missing friend, are you sure that you didn't catch the detective bug—maybe you want to get a chance to do a little investigating yourself."

Marie sighed. "After what I went through in England last year, I'm happy to leave the detecting to Jeremy. Of course, if an idea came to mind, I would share it with him—"

"Aha! I thought so," said Allan.

Smith and Marie both laughed. "No, no," said Smith, "really, she's going to help Mrs. Berger. That's all."

"So what *is* your thinking about all this, Jeremy," said Barbara. "Why are you guys still nosing around? Why did you put off leaving an extra day? I still can't believe that Arthur could do this thing, but Bob wouldn't arrest him for no good reason."

"Of course not," said Smith. "But a person's character is also evidence. And when there's a small piece of evidence that doesn't seem to fit the facts, you keep looking just to be safe. Of course, you have to go with the preponderance of the evidence, but if there's something that doesn't feel right—"

"And Arthur's character doesn't fit the facts?" said Barbara.

"No, it doesn't, but I'm sure you're not surprised to hear that there are circumstances in life that can even overwhelm people who have very strong characters, so you can't ignore the physical evidence."

"Then there *is* physical evidence!" said Allan.

"I didn't say what there is or isn't in this case. I'm speaking hypothetically. And now, I'm not speaking about this at all anymore. We're going to order a nice dinner and talk about how beautiful Jenny looked yesterday, and how lucky you were with the weather, and how happy we are to have been there and to be spending time with you now."

Barbara smiled proudly. "She *was* beautiful, wasn't she, though."

"What do you mean *was*," said Allan. "She's *always* beautiful!"

"Well, now that we've settled that," said Smith, "I'm ready to order."

"So am I," said Marie. "Let's eat!"

*****

Smith turned his head on his pillow and looked down at Marie lying in the crook of his left arm, her head on his shoulder, her own left arm lying on his chest. He felt his chest constrict, and he reached out his right hand to touch the side of her cheek.

Marie smiled, her eyes remaining closed.

"Marie?" said Smith.

"Yes?"

"You're not going to ask any questions that might upset Kathy Berger are you?"

"What do you mean?"

"I mean, you *are* going to stick to her finances, right? Even if you get an idea while you're there?"

"Of course. You'll be coming there anyway. If I do get an idea, I can wait for you. Besides, this time it seems like you're the one with all the ideas. I have totally no opinions. Why are you asking me this now?"

"I guess I was nervous that maybe Bob was right and you shouldn't be involved with these people at all. I got worried about you for a minute. I wonder if Richard will be there."

"Well, if he is, I promise not to set him off into a homicidal rage. Does that make you feel better?"

"Oh, yes," said Smith, with a grimace. "That's *much* better. Thanks a lot!"

Chapter 27

Penny made the drive into Mountlake the first thing in the morning. He wanted to go over all of the findings with Senior Investigator Jacobs and to decide on a next step, if there was to be one. That depended somewhat on the man sitting in front of him.

"So," said Jacobs. "I see what you're saying now—that *if* the hammer was planted, it could have nothing to do with the cause of death or even with the murderer, and that opens the field way up. And I've told you before that I understand how you don't want to think you missed that hammer the first time. *I* even find it hard to believe that you did, knowing you. But in the long run, we're still reaching here. Especially now that the DA feels he can smell a motive, thanks to Jeremy Smith. What exactly do you want to do now?"

"I want to check alibis for later in the day that Jason died, and the next morning. I also want to talk to the other local men who had argued with Jason over the past few weeks, and to more of Richard's tenants. And I'm not completely reassured that Markowicj was not involved—he could still have been the one to plant the hammer."

"Bob, if the murderer planted the hammer after the fact, it would mean that the murder wasn't planned, so how could Markowicj be working with someone else?"

"It could have been unplanned or it could have been planned to look like an accident, but then Markowicj decided whoever did it needed more insurance."

"Okay, I can see that."

"He, or someone else, might have known who killed Jason and was protecting that person. And in case the hammer *is* bogus, I might as well keep checking out the other leads."

Jacobs sighed. "As long as you can handle the workload, go ahead. I'm not putting any more men on it, though. The DA feels he has a case against Walker. He doesn't mind you closing any reasonable doubt loopholes that might be brought up by a defense attorney during trial, but he doesn't have any doubt himself."

"I understand."

Penny left Jacobs' office and headed for his car. Arthur would be having a probable cause hearing this afternoon to decide whether he should be held for trial. It's doubtful that the judge would set bail in a homicide case. Still, Penny wanted to get as much done as he could before Arthur came before the judge.

He drove back to the barracks. Jimmy was already there, looking at the rental records.

"I've got that list for you, with phone numbers and anything unusual I could find about the tenants in the records. Did you still want me to call them, or will you?"

Penny looked at his watch and scanned the list. It seemed straightforward, except for maybe one entry. "You go ahead and call them, Jimmy. Ask them about their relationship with Richard and with the Berger's, and also see if you can get alibis for the entire day Jason died and the next day. I'm going to start with Markowicj and with the guys who had recent arguments with Jason. Do you mind staying?"

"No, of course not. I'll stay as long as I'm needed today. I know we're shorthanded this month."

"Thanks."

Penny placed a phone call to Markowicj's cell phone and was glad when Markowicj answered. If he hadn't, Penny would have had to make the trip up to the site, something he'd like to avoid. Time was precious today.

"What do you need from me now," said Markowicj. "You caught me on a break."

"Just a couple of questions," said Penny. "Do you remember where you were after work on the day Jason died."

"What day was that again?"

"Thursday."

There was a moment of silence. "I went straight home that day. My wife went to see her aunt in the nursing home, and I had to baby sit."

"So, you were alone with your kids?"

"No, actually. After dinner, my wife left, and I took the kids over to my in-laws. We all watched a movie. Then Janie—my wife—came there from the nursing home and we all slept over."

"And the next morning?"

"It was an early day also. I left for work at five-thirty and got there at six. There were people there before me, so they can verify the time if you need to know that. Why do you have to ask about all this?"

"I'm just tying up some loose ends. Thanks for your help. That's it for now."

"No problem, but I can't imagine anything else I could possibly help you with, so I hope that's it, period. Goodbye, Investigator Penny."

"Goodbye."

Penny sighed. It wasn't that he wanted to put Markowicj in Arthur's place. That was as bad as whoever may have framed Arthur, *if* he was framed. It's just that the coincidence of his being on both lists—being an ex-tenant and having argued with Jason recently—seemed important.

Still, the two facts were related, so that's not such a big coincidence, and it may be that he wasn't involved in Jason's death.

Jimmy was on the phone already, so Penny just waved at him, grabbed a muffin from the desk on his way out, and headed for his car. His next stop was Tony's bookstore. Tony was just finishing up with a customer when Penny arrived. Penny looked at a few book titles on a shelf until the customer left, and then walked over to Tony.

"Hi, Bob. What can I do you for?"

Penny kept his face neutral. "I'm here officially, Tony. I'm just tying up some loose ends in Jason's death—to get a bigger picture. I hear that Jason wasn't himself for a couple of weeks before he died, and that you may have witnessed some of this."

Tony frowned. "I don't like to talk badly about someone behind their back, alive or dead."

"I know that," said Penny. "I need to hear it, though."

Tony sighed. "It wasn't much. He came in here to buy one of the puzzle books that Kathy likes, but I didn't have any new ones in yet. He just went crazy, yelling at me that I was a selfish SOB who didn't care about the local people, and that all I cared about were the f-ing tourists. That kind of thing. Ella came in just then and told him to calm down and watch his language. I thought she was going to box his ears."

Tony and Penny both laughed.

"Anyway, he stopped immediately. He just turned and left. It surprised me because I really thought he was too far gone to listen to reason. I should have known—the power of the library! He's been going there since he was a little kid, so Ella has clout."

"I'm surprised Ella never mentioned this incident to me," said Penny.

"She didn't? Then who told you about it?"

Penny didn't answer.

"Well," continued Tony, "why would she, really. Unless she wanted to imply I was mad enough at him to kill him, which would be stupid." He paused. "Hey, is that what you're checking out?"

"Not necessarily. I need to understand Jason's frame of mind."

"Hm. Well, if she didn't tell you, she must have told other people about it. I guess that's how you heard. And anyway, I felt bad for him and made sure to get the new books in. I brought one to Kathy myself two days later, no charge."

"That was kind of you, and good business too. Thanks for clearing it up."

"No problem."

"Oh, one more thing. I know you were here in the store when he died. Where were you the rest of the day?"

Tony wrinkled his forehead. "Let me think. I closed up at five. My wife met me down here, and we had an early dinner next door. We're painting the inside and the outside of the house, and the fumes make it hard to enjoy a meal. Or to sleep, even. We stayed overnight at Carol and Tom's up the road—do you know them?"

Penny nodded. "And the next morning?"

"We went back home and opened up all the windows again. Then I came back here. Hey, you were here that day, with Jeremy Smith's wife."

"Marie."

"Yeah, Marie."

"And when you were out and about, did you see anything unusual?"

"No. And I think I'd remember, because of Jason's death and all."

"Okay, thanks again."

Penny left and went to the library. It was the easiest part of the story to check. He'd still need to talk to Tony's wife and to Carol and Tom. Ella was at the desk.

"Hi, Bob," she said. "Can I help you?"

"I just wanted to ask you about how Jason was acting in the bookstore. You didn't mention it."

She looked blankly at him for a second, and then the light came on. "Oh, that. It wasn't anything. Except it wasn't like Jason to show his temper anymore. He had a big one for a short time as a child, after his father died, but then he became as calm and mild-mannered as you please. It did get me to thinking, though. Beth told me he'd broken up with her, but he was acting more like someone who had lost something he *wanted* to keep."

Penny made a mental note of the further confirmation of the breakup, and of the fact that Beth had told Ella it was Jason who broke it off.

"I see. Okay, thanks. Oh, is there anything else unusual you can remember, now that we're talking about it, before Jason died?"

"There's always something unusual going on with someone around here. But if you mean about Jason ... well, all I can think of is he may have had a little tiff with Karl at the pharmacy also, but I wasn't there."

"Yes, that's where I'm headed next. Thanks."

Penny drove the two blocks to the pharmacy in deep thought. Jason was obviously in pain and acting out. Who knows *who* he might have angered? But that included Arthur.

Karl's wife, Bonny, was at the counter.

"Hi, Bonny. Is Karl in?"

"Hi, Bob. He's in back, filling prescriptions."

"I need to ask him something. Official business."

"Go on back." She turned and called out, "Karl, Bob Penny's coming back to ask you something."

"Thanks." Penny smiled and went behind the counter. He found Karl Parks sitting on a stool at a tall table, a small bottle and a large bottle of liquid in front of him.

"Hello, Bob," said Parks. "What's up?"

"I'm just filling in a few details about Jason—how he was acting before he died. I hear you may have something to tell me about that."

"I sure do. It was maybe a week before he died. He had called ahead for a prescription, but we were crazy busy that day. I'm here alone, you know, a lot of the time. I don't have high school kids filling prescriptions for me like the bigger pharmacies."

"High school kids?"

"Oh, pharmacy techs, or whatever they call them. But anyway, you have to pay attention to what you're doing, you know. You can't rush this stuff just because it's busy. You could kill someone. People don't understand the pressure until there's a mistake—then, suddenly, they understand that they're not just buying soda pop here or something. I have to be alert. So anyway, I didn't have it ready for him yet when he got here. He went crazy. Accused me of putting other people ahead of him because I didn't respect him and his mother. He said—" Parks stopped and looked down.

"Yes?"

"Oh, well, I don't like to say ..."

"What did he say, Karl?"

"He said, 'What happened? Did one of the all-mighty Walkers come in here? Did you drop everything for them?' I told him no, that it was busy and his order was next. I have to admit I was a little annoyed and told him he could wait his turn like everyone else and get the chip off his shoulder."

"What did he say then?"

"Nothing. He just turned and ran out, cursing to himself."

"Was anyone else here?"

"The store was full! I can give you names if you want."

"Maybe later. Oh, one more thing. I know you were here when Jason died, but do you remember what you did afterwards and the next morning, and if you saw anything unusual then?"

"Unusual how?"

"Anything to do with Jason, or maybe Arthur?"

"Not really. Unless, well, I did maybe see something interesting when I was delivering a prescription after work. I have a customer who can't get out of the house. Usually her daughter picks up her prescriptions, but her daughter's sick. Anyway, she lives out past the Walker house."

Penny's ears perked up. "So you were driving out past the Walker's house after work on Thursday?"

"Yes, that's what I'm telling you, if you'll let me. So all I'm saying is that I saw Kathy Berger's pickup truck parked in that little pullover spot just past the Walker house. I remember thinking at the time that I was surprised she was out and about, given her loss. And then, the next day, when you arrested Arthur, it seemed interesting that she should have been there."

Bob had felt his eyes widen as he listened to what Parks had to say. It was Mrs. Berger's truck, but who was driving it? He looked at his watch. He knew Marie was at the Berger house, and that Jeremy would be arriving there around 3:00 PM. He'd wait until then. Meantime, there was one more stop to make. He said his goodbyes and headed for the post office. When he got there, Warren Schell was on his way out the door.

"Warren, can you give me a minute," Penny called out from his car.

Warren stopped and waved. "Hi, Bob, sure."

Penny parked his car. "Where are you off to?"

"Just my usual lunchtime walk."

"Hop in," said Penny.

Warren joined Penny in the front of the car. "So, what's up?" he asked.

"I'm just tying up some loose ends about Jason Berger's death, and I hear he wasn't himself the last couple of weeks."

Warren looked upset. "No, he wasn't."

"Did you see something, Warren?"

Warren hesitated. "I guess you can hear about it from someone else if I don't tell you. I know him pretty well—at least I thought I did. We were tight in school. I … I know for a fact that he valued my friendship. That's what makes it even stranger that he would give me such a hard time."

"What happened?"

"Oh, he was upset because he missed a package delivery, and the note in his box said he could pick it up here after three, but it wasn't here yet. He couldn't wait, and he wanted me to make Lisa deliver it again the same day—drive all the way back out there—because it was her fault that she wasn't back yet. I tried to explain that she couldn't do that, but maybe *I* could bring it to him. He was adamant that it had to be her. He started yelling about people taking responsibility for their own actions. I just got mad and told him that, just because things didn't work out with Beth, he didn't need to take it out on everyone else."

"Wow, what did he say to that?"

"He stopped cold. His face got white as a sheet. He turned and ran out."

"And when did this happen?"

Warren looked down for a moment. "It was just the day before he died. I never got a chance to make it right with him. I knew how sensitive he was—not everyone knew that. I should have cut him some slack. But he'd been acting like a jerk for days."

Penny was silent for a moment himself. "Okay, then, that gives me a good picture of his state of mind. Thanks. One more thing—where were you after work the day he died, and the next morning?"

"I had gone home right after work. I didn't hear about his death until later that night. Then, I needed to be alone. Up until ... until you arrested Arthur, I felt responsible somehow, like I could have stopped it. Even after, if he had pissed Arthur off so bad that Arthur killed him, I thought that, maybe, if I had helped him to calm down, it wouldn't have happened. His mother must feel even worse, I guess."

Penny was confused. "Well, I guess a mother would feel she could have helped him with his anger."

"That too, I guess."

That, too? "What else is there?"

Listening to Warren's answer, Penny fought to keep his face completely calm. *Oh, my God,* he thought, more as a prayer than as profanity.

As soon as Warren left the car, Penny took a chance and dialed Smith's cell phone. There was no answer, so he figured Smith was somewhere without a signal. He left a message for Smith to call him ASAP, and headed for the barracks. *I'd rather not go there until Jeremy takes Marie out.*

At the barracks, Jimmy was just getting off the phone.

"Hi, Bob. I just finished going through the list of tenants."

Penny forced himself to focus. "Find anything?"

"Not really. One tenant before Markowicj didn't pay the rent for several months before they could get rid of him, but all the others left after a few months for different reasons. One family moved out of state. One lady got pregnant and they needed a bigger house. One family was building their own house, and it was ready. No one had any problem with the Bergers or Richard Tomlinson."

"What about the person who didn't pay rent?"

"He was evicted finally about a year before Markowicj moved in. They moved out of state also."

"Maybe that's why Jason was so rough on Markowicj. He had already had one bad experience. Maybe he didn't want to deal with it again."

"Did you turn up anything?" asked Jimmy.

Penny hesitated. "Yes, I believe I did. Karl Parks says he saw Kathy Berger's truck up near the Walker house the evening of Jason's death. So she or Richard could have stolen the hammer."

"Wow."

"At first, though, I was also thinking that if Karl says he saw the car there, it also meant that *he* was near the Walker house himself."

"Hey, that's right."

"But then, Warren at the post office told me something more." He hesitated again. "He says he saw Kathy Berger pulling into the parking area near where Jason died at four o'clock on the day of his death. Not just her truck—he saw her driving."

"Oh, man! She never said anything like that."

"No, she didn't. And while this also means that Warren was near where Jason died, just like Karl was near where the hammer came from, I can't believe that both Warren and Karl are making it up. One of them at least must be telling the truth, which makes me think they both are. If Kathy Berger didn't say she was in one place, she probably didn't tell us about the other place either."

"So what does it mean?"

"Well, it could mean that she was at the river too late to help, and she feels so guilty she's blocked it out. Or, it could mean that she *did* see Arthur there, and that's why she was so convinced from the start that he did it, and maybe she wanted to put the hammer there to make sure he couldn't talk his way out of it."

"But why not just tell us she saw him?"

"Maybe she was afraid it would be one person's word against another, and it wouldn't be enough without evidence. There's another possibility, though. She could have seen someone else kill Jason—someone she wanted to protect."

"Richard! But if he killed Jason, why would she help him?"

"Maybe if she saw it wasn't intentional on Richard's part—maybe he was protecting himself from Jason's temper—she might still want to help him. Or *he* could have taken the hammer, and she's just not telling us. I have to wonder about something, though ..."

"What?"

"Jason was making a lot of people angry. Could he have made his mother angry that day? Whether by accident or a conscious action, could she have killed her own son?"

Chapter 28

"Well," said Marie, "it looks like Jason kept really good records." She took another sip of the tea that Kathy Berger had provided, and a bite of a cookie.

Mrs. Berger smiled. "Yes, Jason was very methodical. I wish Richard were around so he could hear you say that. He wanted to be, I know. He seemed a little worried about the farm's books, but I knew *that* part was good. I just don't know ..." She held back her tears, but Marie heard them in her voice. "I just don't know what to do now."

"Well, as I said, it seems like your assets are well balanced. I don't know much about the actual running of the farm and the financial implications of that, but if these books are accurate, the farm seems to be doing well. I think the budget we worked out will be a good starting point for you right now. And for a self-employed person, you have more non-farm assets than I expected. You've been putting money into an IRA for years, and your farm, as a business, provides a 401K. That's unusual. I thought farms had to put most of their money back into equipment and seeds and things."

"My husband always believed you had to take care of the people who worked for you. I'm not sure that Jason agreed, but I insisted on that."

"It looks like Jason had a lot of your IRA/401K money in the stock market at one point, but he seems to have sold quite a bit before the prices came down very far, so you're still in a position, eventually, to get a decent income from that money. The problem is, this is money you shouldn't touch for another ten years, and you're wanting to know what to do now. I don't feel I can advise you further. You might want to get a local financial advisor—someone who can become more familiar with your financial profile. He or she can help you consider if it might be a good idea to start putting some of the money, cautiously, back into stocks, at the low prices they're at now, or into some bonds."

"Oh, I know you can't tell me everything to do on such a quick visit, but you've already helped me, and I can't thank you enough. It all seemed overwhelming. At least now I know what's there. I feel like I have a handle on it. I wasn't always stupid about money, you know, even if I didn't do well in math class! I'm just rusty because I had let my brother-in-law, and then my boy ... Oh, sorry."

This time the tears did well up in her eyes. Marie sat quietly until Mrs. Berger could continue.

"Sorry. Anyway, Jason was very clever about these things, and I let him take over that part. The farm was going to be his anyway. He took good care of me also, as you see. There was some money when his dad died—"

Both women looked up as the front door opened and Richard walked in.

"Sorry I'm late," said Richard, walking up to the kitchen table where the two women sat.

Marie noticed that Mrs. Berger avoided eye contact with him, while Richard stared unnaturally long and hard at her. *It's as if she's afraid of him*, thought Marie. *Or am I imagining things? And is he looking at her that way because he's wondering what she may have said to me?*

"Hello," said Marie. "It's nice to see you again, Richard. We met in town. I'm Marie Smith."

"Yes, I remember," said Richard, shaking her hand. "I've met your husband also. And like I said, I'm sorry to be late. My aunt wanted me to be here to help her understand her financial status, and to understand it myself." He sat next to his aunt at the table.

"Well," said Mrs. Berger, finally speaking up, "We're pretty much done. I think I have a clear picture of things for now. I *would* like your help later on if you decide whether you want to work on the farm or not."

Richard frowned. "Didn't you talk to Marie about that. I've already told you I can't move back here. My life isn't here. Much as I'd love to let you keep running the farm, we need to sell it, Aunt Kathy."

"Well, let's not talk about that now, with Marie here. Although she'll be leaving soon, I think." She looked at Marie.

"Yes," said Marie, quickly. "Jeremy should be here any minute now. But I was ..." Marie hesitated, but she had to pursue her line of thought. If Kathy Berger was afraid of Richard, she wanted to know it by the time Jeremy came—or at least before she and Jeremy left. "I guess I didn't understand what you said, Richard. What did you mean when you said just now that you wished you could *let* Kathy run the farm?"

Richard looked concerned for a moment, but when he spoke, it was in a very casual tone. "Just that she'd need me to keep the farm going, and I don't want any part of it."

"Oh, I see," said Marie.

Looking over at Mrs. Berger, Marie caught a glimpse of controlled rage. It was quickly replaced by a cold stare.

"Well, now," said Mrs. Berger, "you're letting some cats out of the bag, aren't you? Maybe you won't want to let Marie leave here, now, Richard. Maybe she'll suspect something. Maybe you're afraid I'll tell her what you really meant. Is that what you're thinking?"

Marie looked confused, but she definitely was uncomfortable. There was a tension in the air that reminded her that she had promised Jeremy she wouldn't ask any questions related to the case, although the farm *was* related to the financial discussion. She started to get up, thinking that maybe she should wait for Jeremy outside—maybe call him right now on his cell—when there was a knock on the door. As she was halfway standing anyway, she almost bolted toward the door, saying, "Oh, that must be Jeremy now." She flung the door open and sighed in relief. Stepping back, she turned. "Yes, it's him." Smith followed her back into the room.

"Hello," said Smith.

Mrs. Berger got up from the table. "Come in, won't you. Would you like a cup of tea?"

Marie looked at her like she was the Mad Hatter.

"Thank you," said Smith. "I don't mind if I do."

"Actually," said Marie, "I have some things to do to get ready to leave—"

"Oh, I think there's time for one cup," said Smith.

Marie's heart sunk. She wanted to leave, but she couldn't think of a way out. She returned to the table, which now sat four.

*****

Smith watched Marie sit down, hiding his confusion. *What was that about?*

"Have you heard anything?" Mrs. Berger asked Smith after pouring him out a cup of tea.

"No, actually," said Smith. "I believe Arthur's hearing is late this afternoon. They have to have a hearing within seventy-two hours to show that there's enough evidence to hold him. I'm told they don't expect bail to be granted in a homicide case. So I'm guessing you'll know more about a trial date later today or tomorrow."

"I see," said Mrs. Berger. She started to cry softly again.

"Aunt Kathy," said Richard. "Here." He handed her a tissue. "Why do you have to ask about these things if it upsets you so much?"

"Why! Because the pain of losing Jason is too much to bear. It's just too much. It's suffocating me. And sometimes it feels like the only time I can breathe—the only time I don't feel the pain—is when I'm feeling my anger at Arthur and Beth. That's why!"

Why Beth? thought Smith. *But I understand what she means. And this is a good opening to test my idea.*

"I think I know what you mean," said Smith, softly. "I lost my brother and my parents within a month of each other. My father ..." Even now, Smith had to pause before he said it—even when he was using the words in his work. "My brother was murdered, actually, by a robber, and my father was so upset he started drinking too much. And then, with my mother in the car, he drank and drove. Luckily, no one else died but them. I didn't have to carry *that* guilt around. But at first, I didn't want to be mad at my father. It was his own doing—his own weakness—but I didn't want to blame him. I just wanted to mourn him. So, to block my anger at my father, I chose to be angry with my brother instead."

Mrs. Berger had been listening intently to Smith. "Your brother? For what?"

"For being so stupid as to get himself killed, I guess, and for making my father unhappy. You're right. For nothing, really. There was no reason to be angry with him. I was using anger to block the pain of my grief. As to my father's actions, they were his own choice. In the end, I was able to accept that this was his responsibility. And I realized that I was also upset because it felt as if I wasn't enough for my father after my brother died. Maybe that's why I was mad at my brother—a weird kind of jealousy. For a long time, I think I felt like I didn't deserve a happy life myself, and I kept sabotaging things in my personal life, until ..." He looked over at Marie and smiled. She smiled back.

"Well, I don't think I see the similarity," said Mrs. Berger. She looked more frightened than angry when she said this. "I have a *reason* to be angry with Arthur. He killed my son."

Smith sighed. He also noted that she didn't mention being angry with Beth this time, when she would have had to come up with an explanation for it. He started again, this time more directly.

"I heard that you and your husband were very much in love. That you were inseparable."

"Yes," said Mrs. Berger. "We were. He was a good man. We were best friends—we did everything together."

"So," said Smith, "you must know then, somewhere inside yourself, that if Beth and Arthur feel the same way, it's right that they be together."

Smith saw a light go on in her eyes, but it only lasted a moment before it turned off again.

"No!" she cried out, in a wail. "No!"

Just then, there was a knock on the door. Mrs. Berger jumped up. "I think it's best if you both leave now, if you wouldn't mind." She went to the door and pulled it open, slamming it back into the wall.

*****

Penny looked at Mrs. Berger in surprise. When she flung open the door, she was all flushed and had obviously been crying.

"Oh, no!" she cried out. "And two *more* of you, now! What is it? Can't you all leave me alone?"

Penny didn't look back at Jimmy, who was standing behind him. He kept his eyes focused on Kathy Berger. "I'm sorry, Mrs. Berger," said Penny, gently but firmly. "I need to talk to you."

She looked closely at him and then stepped back, resigned, and returned to the table.

Penny motioned for Jimmy to follow him, and they entered the house.

"Oh," said Penny. "Jeremy and Marie, hello. I saw your car outside. I thought you'd be gone by now. And Richard."

Richard nodded.

"Hi, Bob, Jimmy," said Smith, standing and putting his hand on Marie's shoulder.

"I'd like to speak with Mrs. Berger privately, if you don't mind, Jeremy," said Penny. "If you and Marie could step out—"

"No!" Mrs. Berger practically shouted it. "I ... I'd like them to stay. Please!" She looked pleadingly into Smith's eyes, and then over at Marie.

Smith looked over at Penny. Penny nodded, and then tilted his head back toward the door.

"Okay," said Smith. "We'll wait over there, out of the way." Marie stood up, and they both walked back behind Penny and Jimmy, toward the door.

"What's all this about?" asked Richard.

Penny looked at Richard and then at Mrs. Berger, who hesitated at first but then said, "Him too. I want him to stay."

Mrs. Berger sat down at the table, but not right next to Richard. She kept him behind her, out of her line of vision. Jimmy walked around and stood next to Richard's seat.

Penny also remained standing. He watched Mrs. Berger's eyes look up at his and was surprised to see defiance there. "I have to tell you, and you also, Richard, that you don't have to talk to me now, but if you do, whatever you say can and will be used against you in court. You can talk to an attorney first, and if you can't afford one, we can get you one. Do you understand this?" Penny's voice was very gentle despite the nature of the words he was speaking.

"Of course," said Mrs. Berger, sounding more irritated than concerned.

Penny looked over at Richard, who nodded. "But what's this about?"

Penny ignored Richard's question and began again, still very gently. "Mrs. Berger, I spoke with Karl Parks, the pharmacist in town."

"I know who Karl is, Bob. *You're* the newcomer here, making out like you're something special."

Penny kept his face impassive. "Karl was dropping off a prescription to an elderly neighbor of the Walkers on the evening of the day that Jason died."

It was brief, but Penny saw it. A flicker of concern. It was gone quickly, but so was the defiance that had been in Mrs. Berger's eyes.

"Yes, so…?" she said.

"So he saw your pickup a short distance past their driveway, pulled over in the turnout. He slowed down to see if you needed help. You weren't in it. You never mentioned to us that you were near Arthur's house that night."

"I don't know that I was. It may have been someone else's truck. I'm not the only one in town that drives a green pickup."

"No, he was sure it was yours."

"Aunt Kathy, don't say anything. Say nothing." Richard's voice was low but very firm, each word enunciated slowly and clearly. It held no emotion.

Mrs. Berger hesitated, but she didn't respond to Richard. Instead, she continued. "Well, I can't say. I was in shock that day. I don't know where I may have driven." She seemed less sure of herself.

"Okay. But also, there's something else."

She looked up at him quizzically.

"Warren, at the post office, got off work early the day Jason died. He was driving past the turnoff to the parking area where Jason's pickup was found, right around four o'clock. Kathy, he saw you turning in."

Mrs. Berger's eyes widened slightly and filled with tears, but this time she didn't speak.

"Aunt Kathy! What did you do?"

"Quiet please, Richard," said Penny, "or you'll have to leave. Kathy—Mrs. Berger—is there anything you want to say to me?"

Mrs. Berger sat quietly for a moment and then nodded. Richard just stared at the back of her head this time, not objecting. When she spoke, it was softly at first, but after a while, her tone became harsher.

"It isn't fair. It isn't fair that my boy suffered so because of them, and they get to go on and have a happy life together. Jason may have killed his own physical body, but they'd already murdered his spirit!" She gasped for breath.

My God, suicide, thought Penny. *We thought of that at one point, but then, when it seemed like murder ... And how does she know? Is she still manipulating us?*

"Mrs. Berger, are you saying Jason committed suicide. How do you know that?"

She ignored Penny's question. When she spoke again, her tone was emotionless, almost mechanical. "At first, I didn't want people to know it was suicide, so I stuffed all of Jason's things in his boat and pushed it over the falls. I wanted people to think it was an accident. Then later, I started thinking about Arthur. This was all his fault, and it was eating away at me. I remembered that Arthur once told Jason to go to his workroom anytime if he needed to borrow a tool—that he kept it unlocked."

She laughed, almost hysterically, and without any joy in it. "That's when they were buddies. So *I* went to Arthur's workroom. I took one of his hammers. Then I remembered the blood in Jason's bathroom. My baby's blood."

"Blood?" asked Penny.

"I came home and got some of Jason's blood off the sink where it was pooled below the broken mirror, and I put it on the hammer. Then I remembered Richard's book and I decided to get some of Jason's hair from his hairbrush. And I went back ... I went back to where I saw him ... where I saw him—*my baby*!"

She screamed the last two words and then resumed, her voice softer again, less mechanical. "I didn't go looking for him right away after Beth left here. He said he was going fishing. I knew where he'd be, and I could have—I could have gone sooner!"

She looked into Penny's eyes for a brief moment, as if pleading for him to change the past. He had never seen as much pain before in his life as he saw in her eyes before she looked away and continued.

"But then, I was cleaning and I went into his bathroom. There was the blood and the broken mirror, like it had been punched."

She paused again, her face twisted with the memory. There was dead silence in the room as everyone listened, frozen. She continued.

"And I thought about how he didn't tell me they broke up, and I wondered why. I knew I had to go right then and talk to him—not to wait till he got home. And when I got there, I saw him ..." She gulped, gasping for air again. "I saw him ..." Suddenly, she moaned loudly, and shouted, "No! Baby, no, no! Don't jump. Don't! — I couldn't get there in time. I couldn't stop him. My baby ... my baby ..."

Richard jumped up and knelt beside his aunt, who was holding herself and rocking back and forth, crying. "Aunt Kathy, Aunt Kathy." He looked up at Penny. "I didn't know, Bob. I swear. I ... I was suspicious about the hammer because she was so sure Arthur killed Jason when there wasn't any reason to be, and it was crazy how it was like in my book, but I didn't know anything. I'm sorry. Tell Arthur. We're both so sorry. She wasn't in her right mind after that, you must know it. After seeing that! Do you have to take her with you now?"

Penny hesitated, and Richard continued.

"But you have to know ... She hasn't been herself. This isn't her. She hasn't been herself ever since Jason died. She even ..." He paused.

"Yes?"

Richard seemed to make an internal decision. "She even was kind of blackmailing *me*."

"What!"

"I ... well, my aunt had put the farm in Jason's name, and it turns out Jason left a will leaving the farm to me. It never occurred to him that he would die before his mom. My aunt thought that if the police found out, it would give me a motive to kill Jason, and she said that if I didn't stay here with her and run the farm, she'd tell you. And that's not like her to talk like that. That's crazy talk. She's not in her right mind, I tell you!"

"You should have come to us," said Penny. "She could have tried to do the same thing to you that she'd done to Arthur. At the least, it should have made you even more suspicious of her."

"It did, but it was more that I was worried about her, and I put it down to grief. She had to know I couldn't come back here to live. I've always told her how stifled I was here—how I needed to be in a city. And knowing, now, how bad of a trauma she actually had—seeing that! I'm telling you, that's not who my aunt is. She's a kind person!" He hesitated. "She's a person who lets people stay in my rental house without paying because they're having hard times. That's who she is."

Penny hesitated again. He didn't think it was very kind to frame an innocent person, but he knew that this was true about her—she had done it once, and offered it a second time. Maybe she *was* ill. He made a decision. "Will you be responsible for her?"

"I will," said Richard.

Penny sighed. "I think you need to bring her to the hospital. Can you do that?"

Richard looked up into Penny's eyes. "Yes, Bob. I can do that."

"Now?"

"Yes, now."

"Okay. I'll notify Mountlake to get Arthur released. Then I'll follow you to the hospital. And then, we'll see."

Penny put his hand on Mrs. Berger's shoulder. She didn't react. Her head was buried in Richard's chest, and she was still sobbing. Penny looked thoughtfully down at her but didn't speak.

"Jimmy, stay here while Richard gets Mrs. Berger ready. Then escort them both to his car. I'll be waiting outside with the Smiths."

Penny turned and saw Smith and Marie at the door. He nodded, and Smith opened it.

*****

Marie started to follow Smith out of the house, and then paused.

"Wait! Please, I have to …"

Marie walked back to Mrs. Berger and touched her lightly on the shoulder.

"Kathy?" There was no response. "Kathy, I just wanted to tell you. My aunt committed suicide. We were very close. I wanted to tell you that it doesn't mean he didn't love you. It was just that he hurt so much he couldn't think of anything else. It probably wasn't even all about Beth. Maybe, also, for him, it was partly about his dad. He just wanted to stop the pain."

There was still no response, but Marie thought there might have been a lessening of the tension in Mrs. Berger's shoulders and that, at least, she had been heard. She turned and walked back toward Smith and Penny, this time following them out of the house.

Chapter 29

Tuesday arrived. It had been their originally scheduled departure time, but even though the case was solved, Smith and Marie decided they needed a day of rest. Also, Smith wanted to get some more hiking in before starting out on the long drive back to California. Tomorrow would be soon enough to leave. They had spent the morning getting the RV ready to leave the next day, and had just finished lunch.

"It really is beautiful here," said Marie, picking up their coffee cups and placing them in the sink. "After how much we loved Arizona and were thinking of moving there in a couple of years, I never expected to be tempted to move somewhere else."

"I know what you mean," said Smith. "The people here are great also. And it's a more laid back way of life that I kind of like. But you know, Arizona had a lot of the same feeling. It's a different kind of beauty, but there's plenty of hiking. And we can live in a low-traffic area."

"And it *is* closer to California for visiting friends and family—hey!"

Marie looked down. Sparks was poking her in the leg with his nose, insisting on some attention. "Cut it out," she said, and then sighed and gave him a good head rub.

She looked up as Smith began to laugh. Chili Bean was having one of her "look at me—I'm so cute" fits on the floor, lying on her side and flopping around, making funny little noises, rubbing her head into the carpet, and then glancing up at them with a look that said, "Are you watching?"

"I think they need a long walk," said Smith. "But Bob wanted to talk to me today. Maybe we can call and see if he's there, and take the dogs to town. Then we can go to Allan and Barbara's property for that hike."

"Okay. We're having dinner with them anyway, and they've got so much land! And since we're eating out tonight, I've got most everything put away already for traveling tomorrow."

"Sounds like a plan." Smith walked up behind Marie as she started to wash the lunch dishes, wrapped his arms around her, and gave her a kiss. Then he went to get a clean dishtowel out of the pantry so he could dry. Glancing into the bedroom, he saw Pickles lying on the bed, curled up in a tight cat-curl, dead to the world. *He's getting old*, thought Smith.

After they finished with the dishes, Smith got out the cell phone and dialed Bob Penny.

"Hi, Bob. It's Jeremy. Is now a good time for us to get together?"

"Actually, it's perfect."

"We were going to take the dogs for a walk in town to say goodbye to people. Do you want to meet somewhere, or is it okay to bring them into the barracks? Or would you rather we came without them?"

"No, bring them here. I'd like to see *them* too. And Marie of course. I just had the pleasure of seeing Arthur and Beth strolling down the street, holding hands. He was walking her to work at the library. I look forward to continuing that theme and seeing another happy family unit."

Smith smiled. "Great. We'll be right there."

As usual, once they got the dogs' harnesses on for their car seats, there was no containing them. They were very good at listening except on three occasions—when Jeremy or Marie were coming home, when someone was walking right by the house with a dog, or when they knew they were going for a car ride. Then, they wouldn't stop barking. But they settled down again once they were in the car, and rarely barked again—thanks to the dog training class he and Marie had taken with them.

Smith thought about how far they all had come together. Of course, he and the dogs had known and loved each other already before he took them in, which made the transition easier. Chili and Sparks had been more his friend's husband's dogs than hers, and maybe because she and her husband's relationship had been a difficult one, she just couldn't bring herself to keep them after he died. But the dogs knew and trusted Smith, and as soon as he got that house with a yard up in Sonoma County, she gave them to him. They had bonded really quickly with Marie also.

As they approached the town, Marie touched Smith's arm. "Jeremy, let's stop at the observation deck first. I want to look at the river again."

Smith nodded. He passed the left turn to the barracks and pulled into a parking spot adjoining the overlook. Leaving the dogs in the car, they walked to the railing and joined hands, both gasping as a bald eagle flew right over their heads. They looked at each other and smiled.

"Good call," said Smith.

After another moment of silent appreciation, they got back in the car and drove to the barracks. Each attaching one leash to one dog, they went inside.

"Hi," said Bob.

"Hi," said Smith, who was in the lead with Sparks. He looked around. "Where's Jimmy?"

"He's off today. I'm just finishing up some paperwork myself, then I'll be in Mountlake this afternoon."

Marie smiled as Chili Bean ran up to Penny and wagged her tail, letting him pet her. "She likes you."

Bob pointed to the conference table, and they all wandered over and sat down. Sparks sat at their feet, his head on Smith's foot, and Chili Bean jumped up onto Marie's lap.

"So," said Bob, "are you both ready to get out of this place? It wasn't much of a vacation."

"No," said Marie, "we love it here. And the wedding was great, which was the main reason for the visit anyway. But I'm dying to hear how Arthur is doing. How did he and Beth react to everything?"

"They're both relieved, of course. Beth cried when Arthur called her. I gave him a ride back to town after the judge ordered his release. They didn't say a word when they saw each other—they were frozen, staring into each other's eyes for what seemed like forever before they reached for each other and just held on. It was pretty powerful stuff—maybe more so without the words. I left right away."

"What about Kathy Berger?" asked Smith.

"Richard took her straight to the hospital in Mountlake. They have a psychiatric wing. You know, I'm still not a hundred percent sure she shouldn't be charged for what she put Arthur through. I know it's up to the DA to decide, and I guess they're gonna have a bunch of doctor's trying to figure out if she's capable of standing trial. If it weren't for the fact that *everyone* says this isn't like her and that something is wrong … Anyway, Jason's funeral is tomorrow. Richard dealt with the details, and I don't know if she'll even be there."

"When I was at her house," said Marie, "before Jeremy got there, I sensed this tension between her and Richard. I thought she might have been afraid of him—maybe even because she thought he killed Jason. *I* was afraid of him. And the dogs liked her and didn't like Richard, when we met in town once. But I guess it was all about this blackmailing thing and about Jason's will."

"When you think about what Kathy saw, though!" said Bob. "To actually see your child commit suicide and not be able to stop him. That's how Arthur and Beth are looking at it, anyway. They definitely don't plan on any civil suit. I'm glad she cracked like she did, though, or we still might not be sure if it were her or Richard. I think your talking with her right before we got there, Jeremy, must have done something. Maybe you *did* get through to her."

"I hadn't told you what my idea was yet, but I was thinking we were overlooking Kathy Berger. Not in the way that she may have been covering up for Richard—we did think about that possibility—but that she may have been more directly involved herself. I even thought briefly that Jason's death might have been an accident all along and that her anger at Arthur and Beth might have convinced her it was murder and made her frame Arthur. I never thought she'd know for sure that it *wasn't* murder and still frame him."

"It's even hard to believe when we *know* it's true," said Penny, "let alone coming up with it as a theory."

"You know," continued Smith, "when I finished reading Richard's book, I wondered if his description of the murder was based on his knowledge of someone's darker side. I was thinking of Arthur or Jason, or even himself. Now I wonder if it might not be *Kathy* Berger who has more than one side to her."

"I don't know," said Penny. "Richard had to come up with *some* reason for the murder in his book. It kind of had to be someone like that, even if he doesn't know any murderers himself."

Marie had become very quiet. She seemed very pale. Smith noticed and reached for her hand. "Are you okay?"

She looked back at him. "I was just listening to you guys, and I was thinking about how you're always talking about motives. But you haven't mentioned yet that there's another motive now that you didn't know about before—Jason's will. I was thinking how terrible it would be if it were really *Richard* who Kathy saw there, not Jason jumping, and she *is* covering for him."

"My God," said Penny. "It's not possible!"

Smith didn't say anything at first. When he spoke, he looked directly into Marie's eyes. "But it *is* possible, isn't it? Lots of things are possible in life that aren't true. People are sure all the time that parents have killed their own children, or husbands have killed their wives, and they convict them in society even when there isn't evidence to convict them in court. And sometimes it may be true, but sometimes it's discovered much later that it isn't, and that they were innocent. And it's a shame that they had to go through years of suspicion for nothing. That's why there's a court of law. It's exactly because lots of things *are* possible that there needs to be evidence."

"And there's none here," said Penny.

Smith turned to Penny and nodded. "There isn't anything to suggest Richard killed Jason. Even if we'd known about Jason's will sooner, we couldn't have accused Richard of murdering him—we'd have been more suspicious, it's true, and especially because he didn't tell us he was in town. But motive alone isn't enough, and if it were, we'd crucify the children of every parent who died by accident and claim they did it for their inheritance. No, it seemed to me, in my gut, that Kathy Berger wasn't faking anything. I'm satisfied."

"I agree," said Penny. "And it was Richard who *told* us about the will. If they were both in on a cover-up together, that wouldn't have been necessary. They even could have destroyed the will."

Marie nodded. "The idea just came to me, but of course, you're right. I didn't think of that. And I agree with you, Jeremy. I think Kathy's confession *was* genuine. It was so real—and so terrible—that I felt like I was there with her."

"Well, anyway," said Smith, with a smile, "I enjoyed working with you, Bob."

Penny mirrored his smile. "You should do consulting for a living. You're good at weaving in your ideas without interfering with official police procedures. I feel like we should be giving you a paycheck."

"No need, but who knows what's in the future. That's not a bad idea. I get the satisfaction of working the puzzle and seeing justice done without the paperwork! Anyway, we're going to stop in and say goodbye to Tony—"

"Tony's closed on Tuesdays and Wednesdays," said Penny. "Many of the shops are in town since they have to be open on the weekend for the tourists."

"Oh. Well, then, say goodbye for us. We'll head over to the library to say goodbye to Ella, and I guess to Beth also. And maybe we'll finally meet Mary Louise."

"Maggie's there today," said Penny. "She's a volunteer."

"Great!" said Marie. "I'm glad I'll see her again. And I'll finally get to see the children's room."

They all stood up, Chili Bean jumping to the floor, tail wagging a mile a minute. Penny walked them out and gave each dog a pat. "Have a safe trip back."

"Thanks," said Smith. "I'll keep in touch."

"Great! Say hi to Maggie for me."

"Will do," said Smith.

They walked to the car and piled the dogs in, attaching them each to their own car seat. Marie got in and looked over at Smith.

"Jeremy?"

"Yes?"

"You'd already thought of that idea about Richard and the will, *hadn't* you."

Smith smiled. "Yes."

They drove to the library parking lot.

"I don't think we can bring them in," said Marie. "Park here. We can see the car from inside."

"That'll work." Smith cracked the windows open. "We'll be quick."

It was Maggie at the counter this time. "Hi!" she said.

"Hi!" said Marie. "We just left Bob. He said to say hello."

Maggie laughed.

"So," said Marie, "it's a bonus that *you're* here! I didn't think I'd see you again this trip, after the wedding."

"Yes, I'm off on Tuesdays and I volunteer until three. Mary Louise and Beth are downstairs finishing up a children's program now, so I keep Ella company up here."

"Did I hear my name?" Ella walked up to them from the stacks to Smith's left. "Hello, you two."

"Hi," said Smith. "We came to say goodbye."

"And I wanted to see the children's room," said Marie, "but there's another program going on!"

"Why don't you just run on down there and take a peak at least," said Ella.

"Thanks, I will."

Smith smiled as he watched Marie head down the stairs.

"Well," said Ella, "I guess we kept you pretty busy, didn't we. You must be glad to be leaving."

"No, not at all," said Smith. "We like it here."

"I heard that it was suicide," said Ella. "Jason, I mean. It's a shame. The boy was the sweetest thing when he was young, but he just never was the same after his father died. I know that he was very wary of getting involved in *any* relationship because of that. He had a real fear of losing someone else he loved, I think, and decided somewhere along the line that it was safer to not love anybody else. Except his mother, of course. And *that* was a surprise, too. I didn't think Kathy had a mean bone in her."

Somehow, Smith was not at all surprised that Ella seemed to know all the details already. *Small-town life!*

"She and her husband were very close," continued Ella. "I sometimes think that the children can feel left out somehow when the parents seem to complete each other so much—like there's no place for them. Or else, it can give them an unrealistic goal for themselves. But anyway, she survived her husband's death, but maybe not as well as I thought. She must have been already damaged somewhat to react the way she did now, even though it's terrible to lose a child. And that book of Richard's—I wonder if he didn't have a sense of the damage there was in that household to influence him to distort Gwennie and Jack's story that way! It might have given him a warped idea of what true love could lead to."

Smith was startled to hear Ella voice some of his own thoughts, and in a much clearer way.

"It was *suicide*, though," said Marie, returning from below. "And Kathy *saw* it!"

"Oh, my, I hadn't heard that," said Ella. "She *saw* it. Oh, my. Well, anyway, people say suicide is terrible, I know, but at least Jason didn't hurt anyone else because of his own pain. I respect him for that. Like I said, it wasn't like him to take the big risk anyway, as he'd see it—to let himself get involved with Beth—being afraid like he was. Oh, here they are."

Mary Louise and Beth had come up the steps from the children's room.

"Hi," said Beth.

"Hi," said Smith. "I don't think you met my wife. Marie, this is Beth White. And I assume this is Mary Louise."

"Yes, hi," said Mary Louise.

"I love your children's room," said Marie. "It's so cute!"

"Thanks," said Mary Louise, with a smile. "And I heard what you were just saying, Ella. I have to say that I think we all take that risk, and it's worth it. After the pain of the loss eases, the love is still with you. You never lose that, and you're better off for it." She plopped an armful of books on the counter.

"I agree," said Beth. "I mean, I agree that Jason didn't know how to focus on the love instead of the loss, with his dad. I saw that with how he needed to try to control things with me. But you know, when Arthur and I were going through all this, one of the things I thought about that kept me going was how Constance never was bitter after Jack died, and how she still had a good life. She never stopped loving him really, like he was just around the corner. But Arthur and I are getting another chance at a life together, and we'll make the most of it. When one of us passes on, I know our love will still be alive with the one left behind."

Smith felt a chill go down his spine as Beth spoke, but he shook it off. They all said a final goodbye, and he and Marie returned to the car.

"You know," said Marie. "I got an idea when Beth was talking just now. Maybe there's a reason for all these déjà vu feelings we've been having. What if Beth and Arthur are reincarnated from Constance and Jack? And this time, they get to stay together!"

Smith smiled. Marie had a much more spiritual nature than he did. He tended to be more practical about things. But he respected her feelings and instincts.

"Maybe so," he said, noticing a sudden itch in his brain that he couldn't quite scratch.

Epilogue

Out on the highway again, Smith finally could relax. No matter what that salesman had said, it wasn't a piece of cake driving a motorhome through city streets, especially towing a car on a tow dolly. Even after a couple of months of experience driving it, he still tensed up in cities, or when there was construction on the highway. But on the open road, it was a joy, except that he still had that brain itch bothering him today. It had started in the library yesterday.

The dogs were in their places—Sparks on a pillow beside Marie's feet, and Chili Bean lying on her pillow in the aisle between Marie and Smith. Pickles was in his place in back, on the bed. And the almost-panoramic view through the windshield was great. Pennsylvania was much more beautiful than he had realized it would be. All that green and water made an impression on someone from Northern California.

"It's beautiful here," said Marie, echoing Smith's thoughts. "I don't know, though, Jeremy. It's so far from my family."

"I know. I think we need to spend a few more days in Arizona on the way home to remind ourselves of what we liked there. That would only be a long, one-day drive to San

Francisco in a car—or maybe one and a half. Family is important."

Marie sighed. "I was thinking about what Mary Louise and Beth said yesterday. That's a pretty wonderful way to look at life. You know, *our* love is just as strong, and it *is* worth it, even knowing that someday we may be apart. It'll always be with us."

"I know," said Smith, with a smile. He reached over and squeezed Marie's hand. Then it happened. Words and music started pouring into his head. *Ah, that's it! It's a song.* Keeping his eyes open for a rest stop so he could write it all down, he let the music soothe the itch in his brain.

One Song for the Memory

Music and Lyrics by Jeremy Smith
(S. Goldin)

Chorus (1,2)
One song for the memory, one song inside my head
One song to bring me back to all that I once knew
One song for the memory, one song that never ends
One song to keep alive the love I have for you

Verse 1
I can't recall how long it's been since I lost you, I don't know if I'll ever
want another love. It's only you I'm thinking of. You were the
wonder of my life, a little piece of paradise. You showed me
how to love, and then you left me. How can I begin to start a
new life on my own without your love to keep me whole. You took a
part of me away and now I'm learning how to pray

Chorus

Verse 2
You used to laugh when I was blue and hold me close and say that you
would always be here when I'm sad to love me and to make me
glad that I was healthy and alive and that my tears were small beside the joy that life can bring to all who see that love is never
lost. And in that love we all can live, and when we're gone we still do
give it to the ones we leave behind. You'll always be here in my mind

Chorus 3
One song for the memory, one song inside my head
One song to sing to show the world how much we cared
One song for the memory, one song that never ends
One song to bring alive again the love we shared

One Song for the Memory

J. Smith

copyright 1993 by Sandy Goldin